Can't Pay? Won't Pay!

'Anarchy, theft, class-war, and bopping the fuzz . . . This particular Dario Fo cracker takes its inspiration from an episode in which inflation-dogged Italian women raided a supermarket, either taking the goods or paying a "fair" price . . . Miraculously, he gives even the wildest gags a political flavour.'
Michael Billington, *The Guardian*

Can't Pay? Won't Pay! was the first Dario Fo play to be performed in Britain, in a 1978 production at the Half Moon. It transferred to the West End in 1981, where it ran for two years.

DARIO FO was born in 1926 in Lombardy. He began working in the theatre in 1951 as a comic and mime. Together with his wife, Franca Rame, he was highly successful as actor, director and writer of satirical comedies for the conventional theatre. In the Sixties they abandoned it; Fo began to write for a wider audience in factories and workers' clubs and produced work which was not only an important political intervention in Italy but has been internationally acclaimed. In 1970 he and his wife founded the theatrical collective, La Comune, in Milan. His work – and the work of Franca Rame – has been performed in England with great success: *Can't Pay? Won't Pay!* (Half Moon Theatre and Criterion Theatre, 1981); *Accidental Death of an Anarchist* (Half Moon Theatre and Wyndham's Theatre, London, 1980); *Female Parts* by Franca Rame (National Theatre, London, 1981); *Mistero Buffo* (Riverside Theatre, London, 1983); *Trumpets and Raspberries* (Palace Theatre, Watford; Phoenix Theatre, London, 1984); *Archangels Don't Play Pinball* (Bristol Old Vic, 1986); *Elizabeth* (Half Moon Theatre, London, 1986); *An Ordinary Day* (Borderline Theatre Company, Scotland, touring, 1988) and *The Pope and the Witch* (West Yorkshire Playhouse, Leeds, 1991; Comedy Theatre, London, 1992). *An Ordinary Day* has also been translated by Ed Emery as *A Day Like Any Other*.

by the same author

DARIO FO PLAYS: ONE
(Mistero Buffo, Accidental Death of an Anarchist,
Trumpets & Raspberries, The Virtuous Burglar,
One Was Nude and One Wore Tails)

Accidental Death of an Anarchist
Archangels Don't Play Pinball
Can't Pay? Won't Pay!
Elizabeth
Mistero Buffo
The Pope and the Witch

by Dario Fo & Franca Rame

The Open Couple *and*
An Ordinary Day

by Franca Rame & Dario Fo

A Woman Alone & Other Plays

also available

Dario Fo – People's Court Jester
    by Tony Mitchell
The Tricks of the Trade
    translated by Joe Farrell

DARIO FO

Can't Pay?
Won't Pay!

Translated by LINO PERTILE

Adapted by BILL COLVILL and
ROBERT WALKER

Introduced by STUART HOOD and
FRANCA RAME

METHUEN DRAMA

A METHUEN MODERN PLAY

This corrected edition with Stuart Hood's introduction
first published in 1987 as a paperback original
by Methuen London Ltd.
First published in Great Britain by Pluto Press Ltd in 1978.
Revised adaptation 1982.
Reissued with a new cover design 1993
by Methuen Drama
an imprint of Reed Consumer Books Ltd
Michelin House, 81 Fulham Road, London SW3 6RB
and Auckland, Melbourne, Singapore and Toronto
Original Italian edition copyright © Dario Fo
Italian title: *Non si paga! Non si paga!*
Translation copyright © Robert Walker 1978
Introduction copyright © Methuen London 1987

Printed in Great Britain by
Cox & Wyman Ltd, Reading, Berkshire

The photograph on the front cover is from the 1981 Albery
Theatre production of the play. (Photo: John Haynes)

ISBN 0-413-16590-6

CONTENTS

The Theatre of Dario Fo and Franca Rame

The son of a railway worker, Dario Fo was born in 1926 near the Lago Maggiore in Northern Italy. He grew up in a village community that included glass-blowers and smugglers, where there was a strong tradition of popular narrative – much of it humorously subversive of authority – fed by travelling storytellers and puppeteers. Gifted artistically, he studied architecture at Milan at the art-school attached to the Brera Gallery; but the theatre drew him strongly – first as a set-designer and then as a performer. His career began in revue which was the spectacular escapist entertainment of post-war Italy with girls and comics (some very brilliant like Totò, whom Fo greatly admired) and glamorous *chanteuses*. It was a genre favoured by politicians of the ruling Christian Democrat party; girls' legs were preferable to the social preoccupations of contemporary Italian cinema. In revue Fo began to make his mark as an extraordinarily original comic and mime. On radio he built a reputation with his monologues as a Poer Nano – the poor simpleton who, in telling Bible stories, for example, gets things wrong, preferring Cain to the insufferable prig, Abel. In 1954 he married Franca Rame, a striking and talented actress, who came from a family of travelling players and had made her first stage appearance when she was eight days old. Together they embarked on a highly successful series of productions.

In the fifties the right-wing clerical Christian Democrat government had imposed a tight censorship on film, theatre and broadcasting. Fo took advantage of a slight relaxation in censorship to mount an 'anti-revue', *Il dito nell'occhio* (One in the Eye). His aim was clear – to attack those myths in Italian life which, as he said, 'Fascism had imposed and Christian Democracy had preserved.' *Il dito nell'occhio* was 'one in the eye' for official versions of history. Presented at the Piccolo Teatro in Milan it was an immense success to which the participation of the great French mime, Jacques Lecoq, from whom Fo learned much, was an important contribution. *Il dito nell'occhio* was the first in a series of pieces which drew on French farce, on the traditional sketches of the Rame family, and on the traditions of the circus. This mixture of spectacle, mime and social comment was highly successful but made the authorities nervous; the police were frequently present at performances, following the scripts with pocket torches to ensure that there were no departures from the officially approved text. Fo grew in stature and virtuosity as actor and comic, exploiting his extraordinary range of gesture, movement and facial expression, his variety of voices and accents, and his skill as a story-teller. It was the misfortune of Italian cinema that it was unable to exploit his talents. There were difficulties in finding suitable scripts and, on set, his vitality and spontaneity were denied the space and freedom that the theatre provided. But what Fo did take away from film was an understanding of how montage gave pace to narrative.

In 1959 the Dario Fo-Franca Rame company was invited to open a season at the Odeon Theatre in Milan. The piece they chose was *Gli arcangeli non giocano a flipper* (Archangels Don't Play Pinball), written, directed and designed by Fo. It was unusual in that it dealt critically with certain ludicrous aspects of Italian society. The middle-class audience were astonished by its rhythms and technique and delighted by Fo in the leading role – that of a wise simpleton, who looks back to Poer Nano and forward to a series of similar clowns in later work. Fo and Rame were now securely established both as actors and as personalities in the public eye. Their success in conventional theatre was confirmed by a series of pieces which exploited a mixture of comedy, music and farcical plots in which Fo would, for instance, double as an absent-minded priest and a bandit. The social references were there – Fo and Rame were now both close to the Communist Party and acutely aware of the political tensions in society – and the public readily picked them up. In a period which saw widespread industrial unrest culminating in the general strike of 1960 their material caused the authorities in Milan to threaten to ban performances.

Italian television had been for many years a fief of the Christian Democrats. Programme control was strict: a young woman given to wearing tight sweaters who looked like winning a popular quiz show had to be eliminated on moral grounds. But when in 1962 the centre-left of the Christian Democrats became dominant there was some relaxation of censorship. It was in these circumstances that the Fo-Rame team was invited to appear on the most popular TV show, *Canzonissima*, which, as its name suggests, featured heart-throb singers along with variety acts. Into this show the Fos proceeded to inject their own brand of subversive humour – such as a sketch in which a worker whose aunt has fallen into a mincing-machine, which cannot be stopped for that would interrupt production, piously takes her home as tinned meat. The reaction of the political authorities and of the right-wing press was to call for censorship, duly imposed by the obedient functionaries of Italian television – all of them political appointees. There was a tussle of wills at the end of which the Fos walked out of the show. The scandal was immense. There were parliamentary questions; threats of law-suits on both sides. Fo had public opinion solidly behind him. He had, he said, tried to look behind the facade of the 'economic miracle', to question the view that 'we were all one big family now' and to show how exploitation had increased and scandals flourished. By subverting *Canzonissima* from within he had established himself with a huge popular audience.

During this period Fo had become interested in material set in or drawn from the Middle Ages. He had begun 'to look at the present with the instruments of history and culture in order to judge it better'. He invited the public to use these instruments by writing an ambitious piece, *Isabell, tre caravelle e un cacciaballe* (Isabella, Three Caravels and a Wild-Goose Chaser), in which Columbus – that schoolbook hero – is portrayed as the upwards striving intellectual who loses out in the game of high politics. It was a period when Brecht's *Galileo* was playing with great success in Milan and the theatre was a subject of intense debate in the intellectual and political ferment leading up to the unrest of 1968. For Fo the most important result was probably his collaboration with a group of left-wing musicians who had become interested in the political potential of popular songs. Their work appealed to him because he was himself 'interested above all in a past attached to the roots of the people . . . and the concept of "the new in the traditional".' They put together a show, built round popular and radical songs, to which Fo contributed his theories on the importance of gesture and the rhythms in the performance of folksong; it marked an important step in his development.

In 1967 he put on his last production for the bourgeois theatre, *La signora non è da buttare* (The Lady's Not For Discarding). in which a circus was made the vehicle for an attack on the United States and capitalist society in general. It again attracted the attention of the authorities. Fo was called to police headquarters in Milan and threatened with arrest for 'offensive lines', not included in the approved version, attacking a head of state – Lyndon Johnson. By now it was becoming 'more and more difficult to act in a theatre where everything down to the subdivision of the seating . . . mirrored the class divisions. The choice for an intellectual', Fo concluded, 'was to leave his gilded ghetto and put himself at the disposal of the movement.'

The company with which the Fo's confronted this task was the cooperative Nuova Scena – an attempt to dispense with the traditional roles in a stage company and to make decision-making collective. It was, Fo said in retrospect, a utopian project in which individual talents and capabilities were sacrificed to egalitarian principles. But whatever the internal difficulties there was no doubt as to the success the company enjoyed with a new public which it sought out in the working-class estates, in cooperatives and trade union halls, in factories and workers' clubs. It was a public which knew nothing of the theatre but which found the political attitudes the company presented close to its experience of life. Each performance was followed by a discussion.

Nuova Scena did not last long – it was torn apart by political arguments, by arguments over the relationship of art to society and politics, and by questions of organisation. There were also difficulties with the Communist Party, which often controlled the premises used and whose officials began to react negatively to satirical attacks on their bureaucracy, the inflexibility of the Party line, the intolerance of real discussion. Before the split came, the company had put on a *Grande pantomima con bandiere e pupazzi medi e piccoli* (Grand Pantomime with Flags and Little and Medium Puppets), in which Fo used a huge puppet, drawn from the Sicilian tradition, to represent the state and its continual fight with the 'dragon' of the working class. But the most important production was Fo's one-man show *Mistero Buffo*, which was to become one of his enduring triumphs in Italy and abroad. In it he drew on the counter-culture of the Middle Ages, on apocryphal gospel stories, on legend and tales, presenting episodes in which he played all the roles and used a language in part invented, in part archaic, in part drawn from the dialects of Northern Italy. It has been described as 'an imaginary Esperanto of the poor and disinherited'. In performing the scenes of which *Mistero Buffo* is composed – such as the resurrection of Lazarus, the marriage at Cana, Pope Boniface's encounter with Jesus on the Via Dolorosa and others – Fo drew on two main traditions: that of the *giullare* (inadequately translated into English as 'jester'), the travelling comic, singer, mime, who in the Middle Ages was the carrier of a subversive culture; and that of the great clowns of the Commedia dell'Arte with their use of masks, of dialect and of *grammelot*, that extraordinary onomatopoeic rendering of a language – French, say – invented by the 15th-century comedians in which there are accurate sounds and intonations but few real words, all adding up (with the aid of highly expressive mime) to intelligible discourse.

When Nuova Scena split in 1970 it came hard on the heels of mounting polemics in the Communist press. Looking back, Franca Rame has admitted that she and Dario Fo were perhaps sectarian and sometimes mistaken but that they had had to break with the Communist cultural organisations if they wished to progress. The result was La Comune, a theatre company with its headquarters in Milan. The Fos were now politically linked to the new Left, which found the Communist Party too authoritarian, too locked in the mythology of the Resistance, too inflexible and increasingly conservative. In *Morte accidentale di un'anarchico* (Accidental Death of an Anarchist) Fo produced a piece in which his skill at writing farce and his gifts as a clown were put brilliantly at the service of his politics, playing on the tension between the real death of a prisoner and the farcical inventions advanced by the authorities to explain it. It is estimated that in four years the piece was seen by a million people, many of whom took part in fierce debates after the performance. Fo had succeeded in his aim of making of the theatre 'a great machine which makes people laugh at dramatic things . . . In the laughter there remains a sediment of anger.' So no easy catharsis. There followed a period in which Fo was deeply engaged politically – both through his writings and through his involvement with Franca Rame, who was the main mover of the project – in Red Aid, which collected funds and comforts for Italian political prisoners detained in harsh conditions. His writing dealt with the Palestinian struggle, with Chile, with the methods of the Italian police. In the spring of 1973 Franca Rame was kidnapped from her home in Milan by a Fascist gang, gravely assaulted and left bleeding in the street. Fo himself later that year was arrested and held in prison in Sardinia for refusing to allow police to be present at rehearsals. Demonstrations and protests ensured his release. Dario Fo had, as his lawyer said, for years no longer been only an actor but a political figure whom the state powers would use any weapon to silence.

His political flair was evident in the farce *Non si paga, non si paga* (Can't Pay? Won't Pay!) dating from 1974, which deals with the question of civil disobedience. Significantly, the main upholder of law and order is a Communist shop steward, who disapproves of his wife's gesture of rebellion against the rising cost of living – a raid on a supermarket. It was a piece tried out on and altered at the suggestion of popular audiences – a practice Fo has often used. It was the same spirit that inspired his *Storia di una tigre* (Story of a Tiger), an allegorical monologue dating from 1980 – after a trip to China, and based on a Chinese folktale – the moral of which is that, if you have 'tiger' in you, you must never delegate responsibility to others, never expect others to solve your own problems, and above all avoid that unthinking party loyalty which is the enemy of reason and of revolution. In 1981, following on the kidnapping of Aldo Moro came *Clacson, trombette e pernacchi* (Trumpets and Raspberries). In it Fo doubled as Agnelli, the boss of FIAT, and a FIAT shop steward, whose identities become farcically confused. The play mocks the police and their readiness to see terrorists everywhere and the political cynicism which led to Moro's being abandoned to his fate by his fellow-politicians.

It was the last of Fo's major political works to date. Looking for new fields at a time when the great political upsurge has died away and the consumerist state has apparently triumphed, Fo has turned in recent years to a play on Elizabeth and Essex, with a splendid transvestite part for himself which allows him to use the dialect of *Mistero Buffo*, and a Harlequinade – a slight but charming piece that returns to the techniques of the Commedia dell'Arte.

Meanwhile Franca Rame, who has progressively established herself as a political figure and a powerful feminist, has produced a number of one-woman plays, partly in collaboration with her husband – monologues which are a direct political intervention in a society where the role of women is notably restricted by the Church, the state and male traditions. Like all their work the one-woman plays such as *Il risveglio* (Waking Up) or *Una donna sola* (A Woman Alone) depend on the tension between the unbearable nature of the situation in which the female protagonist finds herself and the grotesque behaviour of people around her – in particular the men. It is a theme which is treated with anger and disgust in *Lo stupro* (The Rape), tragically in her version of *Medea* and comically in *Coppia aperta* (Open Couple) in which the hypocrisies of 'sexual liberation' are dissected.

Dario Fo and Franca Rame have a world-wide reputation. The Scandinavian countries were among the first to welcome them as performers and to produce their work. The whole of Western Europe has by now acknowledged their importance and virtuosity. Ironically the Berliner Ensemble, the theatre founded by Brecht to whom Fo owes so much, found Fo's rock version of *The Begger's Opera* too difficult to take in spite of Brecht's advice to treat famous authors with disrespect if you have the least consideration for the ideas they express. It had to be staged in Italy. Foreign travel has not been without its problems: attacks on the theatre where they played in Buenos Aires under military rule and a visa to the United States long refused. The summer of 1986 saw the American administration at last relent, which may be some sort of comment on how they judge the Fo's impact and importance in the present political climate.

STUART HOOD
September 1986

INTRODUCTION *

by Franca Rame

There are many people who seem to think—perhaps because it is easier and more exciting—that our transition (I mean Dario's and mine) from the traditional theatre to that in which we now work, occurred suddenly, almost overnight, as a consequence of a sort of mystical crisis, as though we had been overcome by the 1968 wave of students' protest and workers' struggles. As if one fine morning we woke up saying: 'That's enough, let's wrap ourselves up in the red flag, let's have our own cultural revolution!'

In fact our true turning point, the point that really mattered, we took at the very beginning of our journey, 22 years ago, when with Paventi, Durano and Lecoq we staged for the first time *The Finger in the Eye*. Those were the days of Scelba and his 'subculture', of Pacelli (the pope) with his civic committees, the days of total censorship. Police superintendents, ministers, bishops and cops understood it immediately: we were 'a company of communists' and we were making 'red propaganda'. Every night there would be an inspector in the auditorium checking our words one by one against the script and the Ministry for Entertainment would obstruct our touring arrangements, while the most reactionary theatre-owners would refuse us their buildings and the bishops would ask the police to tear our programmes from the walls of their cities.

The Finger in the Eye was underlined everywhere we went, among the shows 'advised against' in the parish bulletins. This hounding of 'the communist enemy of civilisation and of Holy Mary' went on for many years with all our shows. However, the workers, the students and the progressive bourgeoisie were supporting us, thereby allowing us to move on and make ourselves known, despite the lack of any prizes.

On more than one occasion we were almost prevented from performing our plays. The opening of *He Had Two Guns*, a play about the collusion between fascism and the bourgeoisie, and between political power and organised crime, was halted by the extremely severe interference of censorship which literally butchered our script. We decided to take no notice of the cuts and get on with the play. There was a trial of strength between us and the Milan prefecture which threatened us with immediate arrest, but in the end the Ministry, worried about a possible scandal, lifted the cuts. The script of the *Archangels* was taken away from us because of the many unauthorised jokes we had added to it during the performance. For the same show we collected 'reports' to the police superintendent of every single town we visited. I was reported for making a remark against the army in a play about Columbus. While running the same *Columbus* we were assaulted by fascists outside the Valle Theatre in Rome, just at a moment when, by a strange coincidence, the police

* Translated by Lino Pertile from *Le Commedie di Dario Fo*, Turin, Einaudi 1975, pp. v–xv.

had disappeared. Dario was even challenged to a duel by an artillery officer, for having slighted the honour of the Italian army, and, crazy as he is, he even accepted the challenge on condition that the duel should be fought barefoot as a Thai boxing match, of which he boasted being regional champion. The artillery officer was never seen again. However, there weren't just funny incidents. Though we were operating inside the 'official' theatre, we were beset by endless troubles and difficulties. The reactionaries and the conservatives could not swallow the kind of 'satirical violence' present in our scripts. Dozens of critics accused us of debasing the stage by introducing politics at every step and they went on proposing the usual, worn out model of 'art for art's sake'.

Our theatre was becoming increasingly provocative, leaving no room for purely 'digestive' entertainment. The reactionaries were getting furious. On more than one occasion there were brawls among the audience, provoked by the fascists in the stalls. The Chief of Siena police had Dario taken in by two 'carabinieri' at the end of a show, because he had offended a foreign head of state (Johnson). Whatever the criticism of our work, it must be recognised that our theatre was alive – we spoke of 'facts' which people needed to hear about. For this reason and for the direct language we used, ours was a popular theatre.

Audiences increased at every performance. From 1964 to 1968 our box-office takings were always the highest among the major companies in Italy and we were among those who charged the lowest prices. Yet it was just at the end of the 1968 season (a true record in terms of takings) that we arrived at the decision to leave the traditional structures of the official theatre. We had realised that, despite the hostility of a few, obtuse reactionaries, the high bourgeoisie reacted to our 'spankings' almost with pleasure. Masochists? No, without realising it, we were helping their digestion. Our 'whipping' boosted their blood circulation, like some good birching after a refreshing sauna. In other words we had become the minstrels of a fat and intelligent bourgeoisie. This bourgeoisie did not mind our criticism, no matter how pitiless it had become through our use of satire and grotesque technique, but only so long as the exposure of their 'vices' occurred exclusively within the structures they controlled.

An example of this rationale was offered by our participation in a TV programme, *Canzonissima*. A few months earlier we had done a show, *Who's Seen Him?*, for the second TV channel which had only recently become operative and was still the privilege of the well-to-do. On that occasion we had been allowed to do a socio-political satire of rather unusual violence, at least by TV standards. Everything went well, without great hitches. Indeed the reviews were totally favourable and we were 'warmly' applauded by the 'selected' audience. However, when we tried to say the same sort of things before an audience of over 20 million people and in the most popular programme of the year (which *Canzonissima*, certainly was), the heavens fell. The same newspapers that had applauded our earlier show now unleashed a lynching campaign. 'It is infamous,' they would say, 'to feed such wickedness, worthy of the basest political propaganda, to an audience as uneducated and easily swayed as the great mass of TV viewers.' Consequently the TV governors, urged by civic committees and by the most backward centres of authority, imposed cuts and vetoes of unimaginable severity. Our scripts were being massacred. It was a return to Scelba's censorship. We were forced to abandon the programme and faced four law suits. For 18 years now we haven't set foot in the TV studios. Thirteen years of 'banishment' and 200 million lire in damages, plus 26 million to pay. Authority does not forgive those who do not respect the rules of *its* game.

It's the usual story. The great kings, the potentates who understand such things, have always paid fools to recite before a public of highly-educated courtiers, their rigmaroles of satirical humours and even of irreverent allusions to their masters' power and injustices. The courtiers could exclaim in amazement: 'What a democratic king! He has the moral strength to laugh at himself!' But we well know that, if the fools had been impudent enough to leave the court and sing the same satires in the town squares, before the peasants, the workers and the exploited, the king and his sycophants would pay them back in a different currency. You are allowed to mock authority, but if you do it from the outside, it will burn you. This is what we had understood. In order to feel at one with our political commitment, it was no longer enough to consider ourselves as democratic, left-wing artists full of sympathy for the working class and, in general, for the exploited. Sympathy was no longer sufficient. The lesson came to us directly from the extraordinary struggles of the working people, from the new impulse that young people were giving in the schools to the fight against authoritarianism and social injustice and for the creation of a new culture and a new relationship with the exploited classes. No longer could we act as intellectuals, sitting comfortably within and above our own privileges, deigning in our goodness to deal with the predicament of the exploited. We had to place ourselves entirely at the service of the exploited, become their minstrels. Which meant going to work within the structures provided by the working class. That is why we immediately thought of the workers' clubs.

The workers' social clubs (*case del popolo*) in Italy represent a peculiar and very widespread phenomenon. They were set up by workers and peasants at the turn of the century, when the first socialist cells began to appear. The fronts of these first buildings used to bear the following inscription: 'If you want to give to the poor, give five coppers, two for bread and three for culture', and culture does not only mean being able to read and write, but also to express one's own creativity on the basis of one's own world-view.

However, by working in these places, we realised that the original need to study and produce culture together, which inspired workers and peasants to build their own clubs, had been completely dissipated. The clubs had become nothing more than shops, selling more or less alcoholic drinks, or dance halls or billiard rooms. I'm not saying that drinking, dancing and playing cards or billiards is unimportant. The trouble is that nothing more went on there. There were almost no discussions. Some documentary films or little shows were put on, but only as a recreational activity. The working class parties had failed to follow up the needs for creative expression that had been manifested so powerfully among workers and peasants. This failure was based on their persuasion that it is useless to stimulate the development of a proletarian culture, since this does not and cannot exist. 'Only one culture exists' – is what those 'who know' say – 'and it is above all classes. Culture is one, as one is the moon or the sun that shine equally for all those who want and can take advantage of them.'

Naturally we soon found ourselves fighting against this unity of classes theory. In the arguments that followed we often quoted the example of the Chinese revolution, where the Party had shown a very different faith in the creativity of the masses and in their ability and willingness to build a different language and a different philosophy of human relationships and social life. Above all we pointed to the great, truly revolutionary determination of the Chinese leaders to urge the intellectuals towards active political participation beyond any personal artistic interest. The intellectuals were asked to commit themselves totally to class struggle, with the aim of studying the culture of peasants and workers and learning about their needs in order to transform them *together* into artistic expression. These ideas drove the Party bureaucrats furious. They would cling to the usual cliché that 'we must move on gradually, starting from the lowest levels, avoiding any flight forward'. They also evinced a certain mistrust of the workers' intelligence and ability not only to express but also to invent a particular cultural world of their own. In fact the workers' clubs' audiences not only listened but actively participated in our debates and our work.

Now, as I read the proofs of those early plays, I remember our first show at the Sant 'Egidio club in the suburbs of Cesena. We had decided to go there for our main rehearsals four or five days before the opening. We were assembling the scaffolding for the stage with the help of the lads in the organisation (ARCI) and a few workers and students. However, the club members went on playing cards at the other end of the hall, looking at us now and again, but with diffidence. Clearly for them we were a group of intellectuals, mildly affected perhaps by the populist bug, stopping over for a few days to refresh our spirit among the proletariat and then away again to where we had come from. What took them by surprise was actually seeing us working, working with our own hands, lifting boxes, carrying steel tubes, fixing nuts and bolts, setting up the stage lights. What? Actors, both male and female, slogging away? Incredible!

In the meantime a rather serious problem had arisen: voices reverberated too much in the hall. We wouldn't perform in those conditions. We had to first arrange some cables underneath the ceiling and to hang a few acoustic panels. We decided to use egg-boxes, the kind made of cardboard. But it was necessary first to tie them together with string, a job which I took on myself together with two other women comrades. We started stringing the boxes together with the help of some upholstering needles, but it wasn't at all easy. After swearing for a couple of hours trying to get the needles through the cardboard, we noticed that the comrades from the club had interrupted their games and were looking at us, following our work with interest but in complete silence. After a while an old comrade muttered, as though talking to himself: 'One would want a much longer needle for that job.' Then, silence again for a few more minutes. Then someone else said: 'I could easily make one with a bicycle spoke.' 'Go!' they all said. In a moment the comrade was back with ten very long needles. Then everybody started to help us to get the string through the boxes and hang them, climbing on step-ladders, like jugglers, cracking jokes, laughing as though it were a big game. A few hours later there were so many people in the hall that we could hardly move. Even the most stubborn billiard players had come to help us and some women too, who had just come to get their husbands back home.

The ice was broken and their diffidence entirely overcome. We had won their sympathy by showing that we too could work and sweat. In the late afternoon, after work, they would come to help us and when we started rehearsing, they would sit at the opposite end of the hall looking at us very quietly. The old men would silence the young ones, who burst out laughing at our jokes: 'You mustn't disturb', they would say. Then little by little they all loosened up. At the end of our rehearsals we would ask for their views, whether they had any criticism to make. At first they wouldn't unbutton, saying that they knew nothing about theatre, but later they became less shy and began to make critical remarks and give us some advice too, which invariably was as unassuming as it was pertinent and to the point. When we finally got to the opening night, the show didn't just belong to 'The New Stage': it was our show in the sense that it belonged to all of us in that hall, who had built it together. Later on, when we moved to other clubs in the vicinity, those comrades followed us and introduced the show to the local comrades. They went out hanging posters and were always the first to speak in the debates. They supported us, we were their team.

In that first year we performed in more than 80 workers' clubs, indoor bowling alleys, occupied factories, suburban cinemas and even in some theatres. We performed before 200,000 and more spectators, of whom 70 per cent had never before seen a play. The debates that followed our shows were always lively, going on till very late at night. Everyone spoke – women, boys, grown-ups and old people. They all talked about their experiences – the Resistance and their struggles – and they told us what we could put on the stage in future: their history.

We drew new themes and plots from those debates, and we found above all a new, direct language without rhetoric or sophistication. For this reason we were accused of populism, but populists are those who parachute down to the people from high above, not those who are up to their necks inside the world of the people and who do their utmost to learn about the struggles of everyday men and women. And by living with the people we have also been able to verify for ourselves the great truth expressed by Brecht when he said: 'The people can say deep and complex things with great simplicity; the populists who descend from above to write for the people say with great simplicity hollow and banal things.'

However, the debates, the polemics and especially the shows that resulted from them, began to annoy the clubs' managers, not to mention those of ARCI, the organisation within which we all were operating. We held on for a while, but in the end were forced to give up. The tension was causing real rows and all sorts of outbursts against us, in oral and written form – in polemical articles in the *Unita* and the Party's cultural journals. Sometimes we reacted without much dialectical sense, in a confused and fanciful manner. We had very little experience of political subtleties nor did we know how to be restrained and accommodating. Nevertheless today, if we look back objectively, while recognising how sectarian we sometimes were and admitting our mistakes, we must say that we could do nothing else. Had we stayed within those structures, we wouldn't have made a single step forward, we would have been ensnared by a thousand compromises.

The separation with ARCI didn't come easily. There was a further division within us too. More than half the company chose to continue working within the ARCI structures and kept calling themselves 'The New Stage'. We called our group 'The Commune'. We had come through a great crisis, but it had been a crisis towards growth and clarity. Basically there had always been a conflict in the company between two fundamentally different ways of looking at our roles as actors. What were we, militants at the complete service of the working class or, more simply, left-wing artists? The dilemma kept emerging. The latter point of view meant accepting more or less correct compromises, veering towards opportunism, renouncing any vigour not only in respect of our own criteria, but also of our collective and individual behaviour both inside and outside the activity of the group. Moreover, there was among ourselves a sort of self-defeating democraticism that was the first cause of arguments, conflicts and division. Dario and I, while trying to avoid acting as managers, made the opposite mistake. We didn't provide any direction at all for the group. What is worse, we allowed some ambitious individuals who were after 'power', to organise political factions to the point of endangering our autonomy. Therefore, two years ago, at the time of the last break-up, Dario and I found ourselves with only four other comrades, completely alone and bereft of everything – the lorry, the vans, the electrical equipment, including our personal stage equipment – we had put together during 20 years' work and which, on leaving the official theatre, we brought to the company.

Whether those comrades were correct in bringing about the split, can perhaps best be judged from the fact that in less than one year their productions have achieved only indescribable failures. They have been cutting each other's throats, they have broken up again, wasted money, sold or abandoned all the equipment. And now they have broken up for good, they don't exist any more. This disaster does not give us any pleasure at all. It only makes us very sad, as we realise how many comrades, with the ability and the quality of good actors, how many who could have continued working for our common aim, can have been so easily undone by the deleterious ideology which time and again emerges like a tumour inside every company: individualism, the struggle for personal power and all the evils that go with it. But we learned one thing, that this mistake can be fought and overcome only if we tie ourselves even more closely to the working class and their struggles, if we let the workers direct our activity and put ourselves entirely at their disposal and service with the utmost confidence. It is because of this principle, that the mood inside our group has entirely changed: there is no more tension, no more personal arguing.

Well, despite all the problems, rows, conflicts and splits, the positive thing is the result of these seven years' work – the millions of people who have seen our plays, our intervention with purpose-written scripts in occupied factories and cities where political trials were being held (as was the case with *The Accidental Death of an Anarchist*, performed in Milan during the Calabresi-Lotta Continua trial; or with *Bang Bang, Who's There? Police!*, performed in Rome for the Valfuda trial; or our interventions on behalf of Giovanni Marius in Salerus and Vallo della Lucania, in Pescara during the trial of fifty prisoners who had rebelled in the city's jail in Mestre to help the Marghera workers; and many other shows in other cities, when the total takings went to support the striking workers of Padua, Bergarus, Asli, Varese, Tusiu and for a long period, Milan; or the sale of 10,000 glasses from an occupied Milanese factory carried out at the Palazzetto dello Sport of Bologna, which was an incredible event, every comrade, every spectator carrying a glass in his hands.)

The fact that Dario, despite so many internal and external worries (trials, assaults, arrests, attempts on his life), managed to write and produce something like three scripts every year (not to mention all the emergency sketches), seems amazing even to me, though I have personally lived through all these ordeals.

At this point I should say something about Dario's craft as a writer, or, I should say, as a maker of scripts for the stage. Why a maker rather than writer? Because, when he writes, Dario needs to think out and build a stage or, preferably, a sequence of scenic spaces and planes on which the dramatic action can take place. It is also a question of theatrical construction rather than simple writing because his theatre is not based on characters, but on *situations*. The characters become masks, i.e. emblematic pretexts at the service of a situation. The stage moves on by virtue of an action, just as the actor moves by virtue of his gestures and his words. Even the stage props therefore become part of an action. This demands great open-mindedness at the level of stage management. Therefore Dario can allow himself to bring on to the stage puppets and marionettes, masks and mannikins, actors with natural or painted faces. And all this he joins together from the inside with the songs, the jokes, the coarse shouting, the use of noisy instruments, the pauses, the exasperated rhythm – though never overdone, because his style is rigorous even when everything seems haphazard and accidental. Only superficial people can in fact think that Dario's theatre is 'handmade'. On the contrary, it is all reasoned out in advance, written, rehearsed, rewritten and rehearsed again and always in a practical relationship to and with the audience. It must be remembered that Dario studied as an architect and that, besides being an actor and a writer, he is also a choreographer. He always sees the stage (and he insists on this) as 'plan, elevation, foreshortening and perspective'. Personally, coming from a family of actors, I've seen, since I was a child, all kinds of shows being prepared and written, but I have always been struck by Dario's method. He has a constant inventiveness and is always lively and young, never banal and obvious. His scripts are always technically perfect, never boring or tiresome. What amazes me most of all is that when he writes, he always keeps the structure of his text entirely open, he doesn't build in advance a complete framework. He invents dialogue based on a paradoxical or a real situation and goes on from there by virtue of some kind of natural, geometric logic, inventing conflicts that find their solutions in one gag after another in correspondence with a parallel political theme, a political theme which must be clear and didactic. You are moved and you laugh, but above all you are made to think, realise and develop your understanding of everyday events that had before escaped your attention.

This is what I think of Dario Fo as playwright. Many others have talked about Dario as writer-director-actor. I can add something about Dario's behaviour as an actor on the stage. He is always alert, ready to catch the mood of an audience with inimitable timing. For the comrades who work with him he is a comrade up until the end of every show. He regrets his success when it compromises that of other actors and he does his utmost to make sure that each one achieves adequate personal satisfaction. If a comrade misses a burst of laughter, he goes on working at it and isn't satisfied until the colleague gets it back.

About Dario the man and partner I am reluctant to say anything, except that his honesty and his inner beauty can be seen better on his face as he grows older. He is getting more gentle, nice and calm, humble, generous and patient. I don't know anybody with so much patience, especially with those who pester him, and god knows how many of them we have met in these years. Moreover, he is generous and stubborn. Nothing depresses him, I've never heard him say 'let's give up'. Even the hardest ordeals, such as my kidnapping by the fascists, or the 1972 split, he has overcome by reasoning with his usual strength, confident that he would make it, trusting the support and the respect of the comrades who have followed us by the thousands. What would you say? Do you think that I am quite 'crazy' about Dario? That I admire him a lot? Too much? Well, I say that yes, I admire him, but even more, I respect him. I was so lucky to meet him! If I hadn't already done it, I'd marry him now.   Franca Rame

This adaptation of **Can't Pay? Won't Pay!** was commissioned by Omega Stage and first presented at the Criterion Theatre, London on 15 July 1981. The cast was as follows:

Antonia	Nick Bartlett
Margherita	Karen Dury
Giovanni	Alfred Molina
Sergeant/Inspector/	Sylvestre McCoy
Old Man/Undertaker	
Luigi	Christopher Ryan

On 19 April 1982 the cast changed as follows:

Antonia	Paolo Dionisotti
Margherita	Lizzie Queen
Giovanni	Christopher Ryan
Sergeant/Inspector/	Nick Edmett
Old Man/Undertaker	
Luigi	Michael Burlington
Adapted & directed by	Robert Walker
Designed by	Geoff Rose

Produced by Ian B. Albery for Omega Stage Limited, Albery Theatre, St Martin's Lane, London WC2.

The first two scenes of Act 2 may be transposed at the Director's discretion.

We Can't Pay? We Won't Pay! was first produced at the Half Moon Theatre on 22 May 1978. The cast was as follows:

Antonia	Frances de la Tour
Margherita	Patti Love
Giovanni	Christopher Malcolm
Sergeant/Inspector/	Matthew Robertson
Old Man/Undertaker	
Luigi	Denis Lawson
Directed by	Robert Walker
Designed by	Mary Lawton, Lolly Hahn (students of the Central School of Art and Design)

ACT 1

The living room and kitchen area of an old, worn second-floor flat in a tenement block. It is clean and neat.

The door bangs open and ANTONIA *staggers in breathless and burdened with four or five plastic bags overflowing with food.* MARGHERITA *follows, likewise breathless and even more heavily burdened with shopping.*

Antonia Blimey, home at last. My feet are killing me. I'll never get use to those stairs. Thank goodness I met you Margherita.

Margherita Christ, Antonia, what happened? Where did you get all this stuff? Won the pools have you?

Antonia That's right.

Margherita Come off it.

Antonia No, tell a lie. I got it all with Green Shield stamps.

Margherita Pull the other one.

Antonia Alright I'll come clean. I swopped it for a two for the price of one off peak return to Florence. It came with the coupon with the cornflakes.

Margherita What Brekki Wheat?

Antonia No. After Germ.

Margherita Get away.

Antonia All right, seeing as you're my best friend, and you keep it to yourself, I've got a rich lover.

Margherita That's it. I'm off.

Antonia Where are you going?

Margherita Home.

Antonia Come on then. Shut the door. I was only kidding.

Margherita Is this going to be one of your stories?

Antonia Margherita how could you. This is not a story. This is an epic.

Margherita Right, out with it then.

Antonia You're not going to believe this. I went to the supermarket as usual and there were a load of women making an almighty row about the prices going up again.

Margherita What's new?

Antonia Well, quite. I mean, spaghetti, sugar, bread, cheese, macaroni.

Margherita Never mind meat and butter.

Antonia Where was I?

Margherita Anchovies.

Antonia No, I wasn't. Oh yes, anyway, everyone shouting the odds about the price of things, and the manager's trying to be reasonable and calm everyone down.

Margherita How'd he do that?

Antonia Shouting his brains out and snatching bog rolls out of people's baskets.

Margherita O, very calming. Very reasonable.

Antonia Well, quite. 'It's not my fault,' he kept saying. 'It's head office. They decide the increases. They're dictated by market forces.' 'We're the market forces.' 'It's free enterprise,' he says, 'competition.' 'Competition?'

I says. 'Competition? Can we enter?' So everyone starts, don't they? 'Competition?' Where's my entry form?' Then this big woman starts. You know her, Mrs Manzi.

Margherita Mrs Manzi?

Antonia Yeah you know. Big woman. Wears a big hat. Spanner in her hand-bag.

Margherita Ah Mrs Manzi.

Antonia Well she says 'We've had enough. From now on we decide the prices. We'll only pay a fair price and no more. And you don't like it we'll nick the stuff.'

Margherita Ooooer.

Antonia 'Hang on,' I said, 'hang on Mrs Manzi'. 'Nick? Nick?' I say. 'Leave it out, we'll liberate the stuff.' 'You're mad the lot of you', says the manager, going red as a beetroot.

Margherita Did you get some?

Antonia No, they looked a bit raddled. By now he's surrounded by women, so he starts to push. Well, that was it! A woman falls down. Then Mrs Manzi yells, 'Coward, attacking a pregnant woman, if she loses her baby, we know who's to blame.' Then I start, don't I? 'Murderer, pervert, paediatrician!'

Margherita I wish I'd been there. What happened then?

Antonia What do you think? He copulated immediately. We all paid exactly what we wanted. Some people went over the top, of course. Insisted on taking all their stuff on credit.

Margherita What's wrong with that? I always shop on tick.

Antonia Without leaving your address? No, we're not giving you an address, you'll only give it to the police,' they said. 'Isn't business based on trust?' they said, 'Well, you'll have to trust us. Ta Ta.' Just then someone shouted 'Police!' Panic stations; and everyone made for the door.

Margherita Oh my good lord!

Antonia Lucky, it was a false alarm.

Margherita Thank God for that.

Antonia Some workers from the factory opposite told us not to worry about the police. 'It's your right to pay your own price. It's like a strike.' They said. 'In fact, it's better than a strike. Instead of the workers losing out this time the bosses lose out.'

Antonia What happened then?

Antonia By now everyone is chanting 'Can't Pay, Won't Pay. Can't Pay, Won't Pay. Doing a rhumba y'know up and down the supermarket and the manager's lying around somewhere and so we scarpered. I came out, head held high, my chest stuck out like a peacock. Everyone's still chanting 'Can't pay. Won't pay!' all up and down the street. It was like a carnival.

Margherita Sod it, and I wasn't there.

Antonia Then the police arrived.

Margherita Thank God, I wasn't there!

Antonia We just stood there rooted to the spot. Not moving a muscle. The cops came running up, and of course couldn't make out what was going on. They're looking for a riot and all they could see was a bunch of housewives loaded down with shopping. For a minute we just stood there. Face to face. High Noon. Nobody knew what to do. Then I said, 'At last you're here. There's a load of robbers in there. Frightened the life out of us. They've highjacked the supermarket.' Then we really scarpered.

Margherita Marvellous. Must have been like the storming of the Bastille or the Winter Palace in Leningrad, and I could have got Luigi his kippers.

Antonia It was a marvellous feeling. Not because we got away with something, but because we were all in it together. Men and women doing something against the bosses.

Margherita They'll be so bleeding scared. Now they'll put the prices down tomorrow.

Antonia Started already, I shouldn't wonder.

Margherita Yea well. Never mind all that. What are you going to tell Giovanni? He won't like it one little bit.

Antonia I'll think up a story.

Margherita Like what?

Antonia You think he'd swallow the off-peak return to Florence?

Margherita Not a chance.

Antonia Green Shield stamps?

Margherita Come off it.

Antonia You're right. That's the trouble with Giovanni.

Margherita What?

Antonia He respects the law. Trouble is I've already spent the money he gave me. I haven't a bean to pay the gas and electric. Mind you, I'm not worried about the rent.

Margherita Why not?

Antonia I haven't paid it for five months.

Margherita Same here.

Antonia Ooh, naughty.

Margherita Oh, I wish I'd been with you. At least I'd have something for my old man's tea.

Antonia You can have some of this. I can't hide it all anyway.

Margherita Ooer. I couldn't.

Antonia Ah go on. Do us a favour.

Margherita Oo no. Luigi'd know, where could I put it? And there's Mama and Papa and Auntie Clara.

Antonia Stop clucking. When you can, pay me. When you've got the money, you can give me for what I've paid for and no more and the rest you can have free.

Margherita Eh?

Antonia Half of this I've half paid for fully, the other half is half free. Oh forget it. Just take it.

Margherita You're forgetting my husband. He's as bad as yours. He'll half kill me if I tell him it's only half paid for.

Antonia My old man'll just nag me to death. 'That's it, cover my name in mud, I've always paid my way, I can hold my head up anywhere, poor, but honest blah blah blah,' until he rabbits me to death. (*Pulls a tin from the nearest bag.*) Hello! Dog food?!

Margherita You haven't got a dog.

Antonia I know I haven't got a dog. Supermeat! What's Supermeat? I must have grabbed it in all the confusion. (*Another packet.*) Look at this. Millet for birds.

Margherita Let's have a look.

Antonia It's just as well I didn't pay for this lot otherwise we'd have to live on frozen rabbits' heads. (*Third packet.*)

Margherita You what? Rabbits' heads?

Antonia Here you are. 'Enrich your poultry's diet with best frozen rabbits' heads.' At least they're the best. 'Two hundred lira.'

Margherita And you want me to take this muck for my Luigi?

Antonia You've got a point. Look I'll take this stuff and you have the rest.

Margherita What if the police search the house?

Antonia There's ten thousand families in this area. Most of them were at the supermarket today. It'd take the police forever to search us all. Sssshhh. Sod it, it's him. He's home. Take this lot under your coat... That's it, so it's not sticking out. (*She starts to stash the shopping under the couch, running between the couch and the kitchen table.* MARGHERITA, *in panic, hovers between, clutching the millet and getting in the way.* ANTONIA *hangs one bag round* MARGHERITA's *neck and buttons her coat.*) I thought you were helping me. Dozy cow. Button your coat. That's it... Help me put my share under the sofa. No, forget it. This stuff in the cupboard, you put that in the sink. Hurry up! Now get going. Act natural.

Enter GIOVANNI, *who freezes when he sees* MARGHERITA's *coat billowing like a bell tent.*

Margherita Oh Giovanni! Hello. How are you? Well, Antonia must be going. Be seeing you.

Antonia Mind how you go, Margherita. Give my love to Luigi.

Margherita Bye. Tra la la. (*Exits.*)

Antonia Tra la la. She can be such a gossip. I haven't the time to chit chat about drinking coffee all day. Have you heard about thingy... What's wrong with you? And why are you late?

Giovanni Did you notice that?

Antonia What?

Giovanni Margherita.

Antonia Yes, that's Margherita.

Giovanni No, I mean, did you notice her... (*He gestures.*)

Antonia Oh that. Yes, that's her belly. Don't worry. She's married.

Giovanni You mean she's pregnant?

Antonia Yes. Miraculous.

Giovanni No. It's a miracle. I mean last Sunday she was this size and suddenly she's out here somewhere.

Antonia Last Sunday is what it is, last Sunday. More things happen in a week. Anyway, since when have you understood anything about women's plumbing?

Giovanni Look, I'm not stupid —

Antonia No?

Giovanni Luigi didn't say anything about this and he tells me everything.

Antonia Everything?

Giovanni About his wife and, you know —

Antonia And?

Giovanni And, well, blimey, we work on the same line. What are you supposed to talk about?

Antonia Maybe Luigi wants to keep some things secret.

Giovanni Secret? What does he want to keep it a secret for? Anyone would want to tell everybody if they were expecting.

Antonia Well, perhaps he doesn't know yet. He could hardly tell you if he didn't know.

Giovanni Doesn't know? Doesn't know?

Antonia Perhaps she doesn't want to tell him yet.

Giovanni Who would she not want to tell yet?

Antonia Him! Luigi! He was always on at her. 'It's too early, we're too young, there's the economic crisis.' And if they found out at work she was pregnant she'd get the sack. So he got her to take the pill.

Giovanni But if she took the pill, how did she get pregnant?

Antonia Maybe it didn't work in her case.

Giovanni Well, she can't help that, that's not her fault. Why not tell Luigi?

Antonia Perhaps the pill didn't work because she didn't take it and if you don't take it, you know, it won't work.

Giovanni Look, hold on —

Antonia You know very well that Margherita is a good Catholic, I'm sure I don't know why. And if the Pope says it's a sin to take the pill, then it's a sin to take the pill and that's that as far as she's concerned.

Giovanni Have you gone bananas? The pill that doesn't work? The Pope and her with a nine-month-old baby? And a husband who doesn't even notice?

Antonia How could he notice it and her all bandaged up like that?

Giovanni Bandaged up?

Antonia Yes, such a shame isn't it, poor soul. Wrapped herself up with bandages just because of him. I told her, finally, if you don't undo them bandages you don't know what you'll get.

Giovanni What would you get?

Antonia (*Thinks.*) A flat baby. Undo those bandages at once, I told her, and stop worrying about your job. Life's too important for that. Well, I couldn't leave her like that, now, could I? I was right to say that, wasn't I, Giovanni? Was I right?

Giovanni Sure you were.

Antonia Have I been good?

Giovanni Yes yes. So what did she do?

Antonia Well, she did as I told her and off came the bandages and out came the belly. Pouf! Like a barrage balloon. Then I told her if her husband makes a fuss, tell him to come over here and see Giovanni and he'll see him off. Giovanni, I was right to do that, wasn't I?

Giovanni Very good. Well done.

Antonia Have I been good?

Giovanni OK, OK.

Antonia OK, OK? What sort of answer is that? OK, OK! I knew you'd have a go at me. I knew it. So what have I done to annoy his lordship now. Don't tell me, I know, trouble at work.

Giovanni As a matter of fact there was.

Antonia Go on, you had a strike.

Giovanni No. It was the canteen. I went up for my dinner as I always do at dinner time and there was a bunch of louts complaining about the food being so disgusting.

Antonia What a shame. I bet the food was really nice.

Giovanni No, it was disgusting. But what's the point of a mass meeting?

Antonia Mass meeting? I thought you said it was a bunch of louts?

Giovanni It was to start with. Then everybody joined in. And d'you know what they did? Everyone ate their dinner and went off without paying!

Antonia Them too?

Giovanni What do you mean, them too?

Antonia Well, I meant not just the bunch of louts but all the others, too.

Giovanni Even, I might add, the shop stewards.

Antonia Well I never.

Giovanni Yes. Shop stewards are supposed to set an example.

Antonia Well, quite.

Giovanni And that's not all.

Antonia You mean there's more?

Giovanni I left the canteen and went for a walk right past this supermarket.

Antonia You mean the one by your work?

Giovanni And blow me if there weren't hundreds of women —

Antonia Yes?

Giovanni Walking out of the store loaded up with goods.

Antonia Yes?

Giovanni And d'you know what they told me?

Antonia No.

Giovanni They hadn't paid for a thing!

Antonia Well, what a turn out.

Giovanni Did you ever hear such a thing? They left without paying!

Antonia Them too.

Giovanni What d'you mean, them too?

Antonia Well, them, just like the bunch of louts and the mass meeting in the canteen. Them too.

Giovanni And, what's more, they roughed up the manager.

Antonia Which, the supermarket or the canteen?

Giovanni Both.

Antonia I don't know what to say.

Giovanni No wonder. These layabouts, these louts, ultra-left extremists play right into the hands of the ruling class. And they'll start calling us decent responsible working men thieves and scum of the earth.

Antonia But I thought it was all women who did the supermarket?

Giovanni Same thing. How d'you think the men will react when they get home?

Antonia No, tell me, I'm all ears.

Giovanni They'll probably congratulate their wives for nicking all that gear. 'Very well nicked, my dear,' they'll say, and off down the boozer to have a good laugh. Instead of... instead of...

Antonia Instead of what?

Giovanni Instead of teaching the wife a lesson. That's what I'd do. I'd chuck the lot at her head then I'd make her eat everything without opening a can, the key and all and then I'd give her a good talking to.

Antonia You would, would you?

Giovanni Certainly I would. So don't get any fancy ideas, because if I found so much as a tin of anchovies in the cupboard that hadn't been paid for or that had been nicked I'd —

Antonia Don't tell me, I know. Key and all.

Giovanni No worse. I'd leave, I'd pack and leave and never come back. No, I'd kill you first and after apply for a divorce.

Antonia Now look, if you feel that strongly about it you can pack and leave right now. Divorce or no divorce. How can you suggest such a thing! Me! I'd let you starve to death rather than make you eat stolen food. I'd let you starve to death first.

Giovanni Right! I'd rather starve than eat stolen food. Which reminds me, I never got any dinner. With all the fuss at the canteen I couldn't risk eating anything in case I got it free. What's for tea?

He sits at the kitchen table. ANTONIA *nervously selects a can at random and puts it in front of him.*

Antonia Here you are.

Giovanni What's that?

Antonia It's good.

Giovanni I know it's good, but what is it?

Antonia Supermeat.

Giovanni Supermeat?

Antonia Supermeat for dogs.

Giovanni What?

Antonia It's very good.

Giovanni It may be, for dogs!

Antonia Nourishing, full of protein, prolongs active life. It says so. There wasn't anything else. And it's cheap.

Giovanni You're joking.

Antonia Who's joking? Ever tried shopping lately? You any idea of the prices nowadays? Everything's double what it was a few months ago. If they stock it. They're hoarding everything, it's the black market all over again. It's worse than wartime.

Giovanni Don't overdo it. Worse than wartime! Anyway, I'm not having that. I'm not a dog yet! Give us a drink of milk then.

Antonia There's no milk.

Giovanni What do you mean, no milk?

Antonia Apparently. Milk's gone up again, so this morning when the milkman came round, a whole bunch of louts — including CP friends of yours —

Giovanni Not our branch.

Antonia — jumped on the float and started giving out the milk at one hundred lira a litre.

Giovanni Did you get some?

Antonia What? Me? Buy half stolen milk? And would you have drunk it?

Giovanni No, you're right.

Antonia Good, then don't drink it.

Giovanni I can't, can I?

Antonia That's what I'm saying.

Giovanni Isn't there anything else?

Antonia Yes. I'll make soup.

Giovanni Sounds good. What kind?

ANTONIA *selects a packet at random and puts it in front of him.*

Antonia Millet.

Giovanni Millet? What millet?

Antonia Millet for canaries.

Giovanni Millet for canaries?!

Antonia Yes. Good for you. Great for diabetes.

Giovanni I haven't got diabetes.

Antonia Stops you getting it. Builds up a barrier. Anyway it costs half as much as rice. Which you don't like anyway.

Giovanni Millet! First you try and turn me into a dog. Now into a canary.

Antonia Well Gloria — you know the fourth floor — she makes it every day for her old man. She swears by it. The secret is in the flavour. Luckily I've got the rabbits' heads and if you give them a good boiling —

Giovanni Rabbits' heads!

Antonia Of course rabbits' heads! Blimey, if you don't know that! Millet soup is made with rabbits' heads. Only the heads, mind you, not the bodies, and they're frozen. That's so they won't rot. Don't tell me you're against frozen food now?

Giovanni That's it. Goodbye.

He starts to go.

Antonia Where are you going?

Giovanni Where d'you think? The caff.

Antonia What about money?

Giovanni Oh yes. Give me some money.

Antonia What money?

Giovanni What do you mean, what money? You're not going to tell me you've run out already?

Antonia Have you forgotten tomorrow we have to pay the gas, electric and rent? Or do you want to be evicted as well as cut off?

Giovanni Course not.

Antonia Well then, the caff is out. But don't worry, I'll see to it.

Giovanni Where are you going?

Antonia To Margherita's. She's been shopping. I'll borrow from her.

Giovanni But no rabbits' heads, please.

Antonia Don't worry. I'll bring you the paws next time. Bring you luck.

Giovanni That's it. Have a good laugh! Go on. Blimey, I'm starving. (*He picks up the tin.*) 'Supermeat for dogs.' Homogenised, tasty. Wonder what it tastes like? Hello, she's lost the key, as usual. Wait a minute. Screwtop. (*He opens the tin.*) Doesn't smell too bad. Bit like pickled jam with a soupcon of truffled kidneys, laced with cod liver oil. A dog'd be a madman to eat this crap. Think I'll have a drop of lemon on top against the cholera. (*Police sirens.*) What's all that? (*He calls out the window to neighbour opposite.*) 'Aldo, what's going on?...Which supermarket?... No, my wife wasn't there! She's dead against these riots, even bought me rabbits' heads to prove it... No, she wasn't out at all today. She had to undo a friend's belly... Not like that! No, she made her undo the bandages... It's her husband, Luigi, he doesn't want her to get pregnant. But she listened to the Pope and so the pill didn't work and she swelled up overnight... You don't understand? Thick burk...' Hello, they're really storming all over the place. Well, if they come here they'll get what for. This is just intimidation, sheer provocation! (SERGEANT *appears in window at rear, clinging to swaying drainpipe.*)

Sergeant Oi! (GIOVANNI, *back to window, shoots arms up.*)

Giovanni O my good God. I'll get shot in the back resisting arrest. (SERGEANT *sways across window again.*)

Sergeant Oi!

Giovanni All right, all right. I'll come quietly. (SERGEANT *sways back into view.*)

Sergeant Oi. You. Desist. (*He hooks a foot over window sill.*)

Giovanni Desist? Desist? I am desisting, aren't I? What more can I desist?

Sergeant Does this flat belong to you?

Giovanni Yes.

Sergeant I order you to assist me.

Giovanni Oh yeah? How? Beat myself up? Punch myself in the nuts?

Sergeant Help!

Giovanni Stop mucking about.

Sergeant Help!

Giovanni What a sense of humour. (*Now* GIOVANNI *turns round and sees policeman clinging to drainpipe with foot in saucepan on window sill.*) I don't believe it. What are you playing at?

Sergeant Help! EEEEK!

Giovanni (*Out front.*) Now that's the law all over. Popping round to do you over they can't come in the door like everyone else. No: door's not good enough for the like of them. Oh no. Tell you what, there was this copper who wanted to get a new pair of boots — this'll kill you —

Sergeant No. It'll kill me. HELP!

Giovanni Don't interrupt. Oh sorry.

Sergeant Get me out of this.

Giovanni What's wrong with the door?

Sergeant Get me out of this.

Giovanni What are you doing out there?

Sergeant It's a search.

Giovanni Oh yeah? Find anything?

Sergeant We're searching your flat.

Giovanni Oh yeah? Got a warrant?

Sergeant IF YOU DON'T GET ME —

Giovanni Alright. Alright. Don't get shirty (*AD LIBS*).

SERGEANT *drops onto balcony and comes through french windows. Goes up behind* GIOVANNI.

Giovanni (*Not realising who he's talking to.*) There's a copper hanging out of the window.

Sergeant Oh really?

Giovanni He wants to come in.

Sergeant Why doesn't he use the door?

Giovanni (*Realising.*) What do you want?

Sergeant It's a search.

Giovanni Where's your warrant?

Sergeant Here's the warrant.

Giovanni What for?

Sergeant What for? What for? Thousands of liras worth of goods were looted from the supermarket today. And he asks me what for?

Giovanni And you dare to come through my window without a shred of evidence? That's character assassination.

Sergeant Call it what you like.

Giovanni I will.

Sergeant Suit yourself. Nothing to do with me. I follow my orders. That's all.

Giovanni I see. I see. All right. All right then, do your worst.

Sergeant Right, I will.

Giovanni But I warn you, this is intimidation, provocation and what's worse, ...it's not very nice. Oh yes. You keep us in a state of subjugation and starvation, then you come round here to take the piss. Look at what I've got to eat. Supermeat for dogs.

Sergeant I beg your pardon?

Giovanni Yes, you see. Go on, have a look. Have a sniff of that. And you know why I have to endure this shite? Because real food costs a fortune. Yeah. And look at this. Rabbits' heads. Get your laughing gear round that.

Sergeant All right, all right. You've made your point.

SERGEANT *looks carefully round the room, then lifting the flap to his tunic pocket, he lifts two inches of* The Little Red Book *out for an instant, then swiftly stuffs it down again.* GIOVANNI *starts.*

Giovanni What's that?

Sergeant All reactionaries are paper tigers.

Giovanni Well knock me sideways with a feather! Sergeant, if I didn't know better I'd say that was a little red book.

Sergeant (*Looks round flat.*) Not a word. (*Slips pack of cards to* GIOVANNI.) That, my old son, is a source of comfort to me on a cold night.

GIOVANNI *perplexed. Fans out cards.*

Sergeant That sonny jim represents the high point of Eastern political thought. If you pardon the phrase.

Giovanni Ace?

Sergeant Precisely. I knew you'd cop it. Well what do you say to that?

Giovanni Four no trumps?

Sergeant (*Noticing.*) Oh sorry. Wrong box.

Sergeant You working classes have got to stop seeing us police as ignorant twits. You see us as creatures of habit with no brain. 'Here boy, down boy, sit, sit, seize him!' A guard dog who can't disagree or have an opinion. 'Heel, heel, lie down, down, Rover.'

Voice (*Outside.*) Sergeant!

Sergeant Up here, second floor! Next floor, lads.

Giovanni All right, I take your point. Maybe we do see you as thick as pigshit. Present company excepted. Of course. After all we all started in the same class. Right? Sons of the soil as we — as the Communists say.

Sergeant Sons of the soil. That's a laugh. Guard dogs for the ruling class, defending their property, their right to exploit, their fiddles, kickbacks.

Giovanni Well, blimey, if you think like that, why did you choose the job?

Sergeant Choose, choose? Did you choose to eat this crap, the rabbits' heads and the canary millet?

Giovanni Course not. But there's no choice. There's nothing else.

Sergeant Exactly. Exactly. My point precisely. What choice did I have? Emigrate, sweep the streets or join the police. What would you do?

Giovanni Must be terrible. But wait a minute. You've got to have the law, after all.

Sergeant Oh yeah? Really? Have you? What if the law's purely for the benefit of the rich? Eh? Eh?

Giovanni Well, then you've got your democratic procedure. Laws can be reformed, you know.

Sergeant Oh really? Reform? Reform? Don't make me laugh. We've been hearing that for 30 years. Reforms. No mate. If the people want change they'll have to do it themselves. They'll have to melt the shackles of capitalism and the iron fist of oppression with the boiling blood of Karl Marx. 'Where the broom does not reach, the dust will not vanish of itself.' Know what I mean? Anyway, Comrade, I better continue with this search or I'll get shot.

Giovanni You see! Blimey, what a turn up. First you're talking like a raving subversive and next you're getting down to your job of turning over innocent people's homes. You kill me!

Sergeant Yeah, well, not today. Look, I'm only human. Obviously, at the moment, at this precise moment I haven't got the commitment and courage and the sheer get-up-and-go. Know what I mean?

Giovanni 'At this moment.' At this moment I know what you mean. You're all left talk. You're all wind, mate. Giving me all this bollocks about having no choice but get into the police and sorry about that, but I can't help it smashing people over the head, but there you go! You should have taken the other road; emigrate or road sweep. Least you'd have your bleeding dignity intact. Know where you'll be tomorrow?

Sergeant No.

Giovanni Beating me up on the picket line. That's where you'll be.

Sergeant You're so right. So terribly, tragically right.

Giovanni Too right. I'm right.

Sergeant But. But. Nevertheless. The police have stood back on occasions, you know. Even dare I say, thrown themselves on the other side.

Giovanni Oh yeah when?

Sergeant Venice Water Riots. August the 5th.

Giovanni (*Impressed.*) Oh.

Sergeant 1723.

Giovanni Oh very relevant. Very topical. I won't hold me breath till it happens again.

Sergeant Ah ye of little faith. But remember 'A revolution is not a dinner party nor is it doing embroidery.' 'The wheel of history is turning.' Well I better get underway. Comrade. (*He exits.*)

Giovanni And good night! Well, fuck a brick! Whatever next. The died-in-the-wool, raving, steeped-in-marxism out-and-out red copper! Right in there with the lunatic fascists, psycho bullies and subnormal everyday street coppers. Well that's where the bleeding extremists fetch up, obviously. In the police! And he's got the neck to stand there in front of me, twenty years a member, and criticise the CP! From the left too! Wait a minute! He was trying to get me going. That's it! That sly bastard. He was just trying to provoke me. Get me talking. 'Assault the bastions of Capital! Rebellion in the Police!' And if I fell for it and agreed with him: Wallop! 'Freeze. Red Brigade. You're under arrest.' Yeah, well, this little fish didn't fall for it. Not me. Not interested in the bait, mate. You'll need a better baited hook to catch this fish. Ah well, back to the dogfood.

Enter ANTONIA *and* MARGHERITA. MARGHERITA *hides behind the door*.

Giovanni What are you doing?

Antonia Have they been here?

Giovanni Who?

Antonia They're searching every house.

Giovanni Oh yes. I know.

Antonia They're already arrested Mandetti and Fossani. They found stuff in their cisterns.

Giovanni Good. That'll teach them.

Antonia Oh very nice. They also took a load of gear that had been properly paid for. I suppose that's good too?

Giovanni Well, that's what happens when unprincipled louts go grabbing stuff at random. The innocent suffer, too. At least we don't have to worry. They've been here already.

Antonia They've been?

Giovanni Sure.

Antonia Did they find anything?

Giovanni What was there to find?

Antonia Nothing. I mean, you think you've got nothing and it turns out —

Giovanni Turns out what?

Antonia It turns out they've planted stuff on you to frame you. It's not the first time it's happened, you know. As they were searching Rosa's son's room — Rosa on the fifth floor — they planted a gun and a pile of leaflets under his bed.

Giovanni Don't be daft. You think they're coming round here planting packets of cornflakes under our sofa.

Antonia Well, I don't know. Not exactly under the sofa, I wouldn't say. It was just for argument's sake.

Giovanni Come to think of it, you may be right! I better have a look.

Antonia No!

Giovanni Why not?

Antonia Well, it's silly, it's daft. What's the point, mmmm, ummm, see? And keep your dirty mitts off of my cushions. I'll have a look. No. Nothing there. See?

Giovanni Well I better check the cupboards.

ANTONIA *squeals.*

Giovanni What was that?

Antonia Margherita.

Giovanni Margherita? Where?

Antonia Outside. (*A quick look under the sofa.*)

Giovanni What did you leave her outside for? What's she doing out there? (*He opens the door.*) Margherita, what are doing there? Are you all right? Come in. What are you crying for?

Margherita Aoaaaooouuu!

Antonia She's speechless.

Giovanni I can see that.

Antonia It's the shock of the police raid. She was on her own at home, when they came storming all over the kitchen. She was terrified. Then this inspector wanted to inspect her stomach.

Giovanni The bastards. How can they — He wanted to *what*?

Antonia He had this mad idea that she had food, packets of pasta and stuff, stuffed up there and she wasn't pregnant at all. I ask you!

Giovanni Callous swine! How do you feel now?

Antonia She's still speechless. Come on Margherita, sit down for a minute. I had to bring her round here, didn't I? I mean, I couldn't leave her.

Giovanni Course not. Let's get her coat off.

Margherita No!

Giovanni She's getting better already. She spoke! Just make yourself at home, dear.

Antonia Leave her alone. She doesn't want to take her coat off. She's cold.

Giovanni It's hot in here.

Antonia It's hot for you. It's cold for her. Maybe she's got a temperature?

Giovanni A temperature? Has she got something?

Antonia What do you mean? Has she got something? Course she's got something. She's got a baby! What should she have?

Margherita Aaah!

Giovanni What's that?

Antonia In fact she's in labour.

Giovanni Already?

Antonia What do you mean already? What do you know? Half an hour ago he didn't even know she was pregnant. Now he's surprised she's in labour.

Giovanni Well, it just seemed a bit quick. You don't think she's premature?

Antonia You don't half go on. What would you know about her being premature or not? Suddenly you're the world's expert and know all about it and, I suppose, much more than we do! Stay there! Now dear, you get under the blankets. And you. Turn round. She's getting undressed.

Margherita No I'm not!

Antonia Ssshhh. There there. It'll soon be over. Don't cry, we'll get out of this.

Margherita How?

Giovanni Mmmm?

Margherita Owoowww.

Giovanni Look, if she's in labour, we'd better get a doctor. Or better still an ambulance.

Antonia Oh you're full of bright ideas you are. We call an ambulance and then drive all round Milan looking for a free bed. You know you have to book months in advance.

Giovanni Why didn't she book then? You get nine months warning with a pregnancy.

Antonia Typical. Of course, it's down to us. Run the house, do the washing, have the babies, and book the beds. And why didn't Luigi do it?

Giovanni He didn't know, did he? What was he supposed to do? Guess?

Antonia Good excuse: 'He didn't know!' Ooo, that's so typical. You give us the pay packet, 'You'll have to manage on that,' insist on your conjugal rights, God forbid you should go without that, then we get pregnant, surprise, surprise, 'Well, go on the pill,' and not a thought for the poor woman who's a Catholic who has double feature nightmares every night, starring the Pope looming up and warning her: 'You're sinning, you know. You should bear children!'

Giovanni Hang on a minute, never mind the conjugal whatsits and the Pope who, I agree is always trying to break our balls too, you know, in our dreams, never mind all that and the pill and the pay packet. When is she supposed to have got pregnant?

Antonia What's it got to do with you? Prying sod! Then he complains about the Pope.

Giovanni No, I meant, they've only been married five months.

Antonia Why couldn't they have done it before? People do, you know. Or are you a bleeding moralist, worse than the Pope? Have you forgotten?

Giovanni Of course not.

Antonia I have.

Giovanni No. But Luigi told me they only made love after they were married.

Margherita My Luigi has told you all these things? My God!

Antonia There, you've upset her with your gossip. Fancy people telling all and sundry the intimate details of their life.

Giovanni I'm not all and sundry. I'm his best friend! He asked my advice because I'm more experienced.

Antonia Oh yeah. What at? Don't answer that.

A knock at the door.

Antonia Who is it?

Inspector Police. Open up.

Margherita Oh my God, aaaaooouuu.

Giovanni It's all right. We've been done.

Enter INSPECTOR, *who is the same actor as the* SERGEANT, *only he wears a moustache.*

Giovanni Oh good evening. Hello, it's you again.

Inspector What do you mean, again?

Giovanni Sorry. My mistake. For a minute I thought you were the one who was here before.

Inspector A likely story.

Giovanni Yes there was. A police sergeant.

Inspector Well, I'm an inspector in the Carabinieri.

Giovanni I can see that, you've got a moustache —

Inspector Are you being witty at my expense?

Giovanni No, no.

Inspector Right. We're searching here.

Giovanni I told you. We've been done already.

Inspector Well, we'll do it again, won't we?

Giovanni Oh I see, you're checking on each other. Then we'll have the customs police, the railway police, the Alpine regiment —

Inspector That's enough of that! We'll just get on with the job.

He heads for the sofa.

Antonia Oh, we all have to get on with that. In our case sweating eight hours a day on the assembly line, like animals, and in your case making sure we behave and — most of all — pay the right price for everything. You don't ever check, for example, that the bosses keep their promises, pay what they've agreed, that they don't kill us with piecework, or by speeding up the line, or screw us with their three-day weeks, that they comply with the safety regulations and pay the proper compensation, that they don't just up the prices, chuck us out in the street or starve us to death!?

INSPECTOR *exits into wardrobe.*

Giovanni That's pitching it a bit strong. Where's he gone? They don't all think like that you know.

Antonia Whose side are you on?

Giovanni Yours, of course, but the previous search party, the sergeant had had a belly full of being ordered about. 'I'm just a doggy,' he said, 'who can't disobey. Down, boy, lie down, Rover.' So they're not all the same.

Inspector (*Emerging from cupboard suddenly.*) What's all that? Rover? Where does this dog come into it?

Giovanni He doesn't come into it at all. The sergeant said we think all policemen are ignorant twits, you see, servants of the most brutal exploiters, catspaws and watchdogs with no brains —

Inspector Right. That does it. Handcuff him!

Giovanni What for?

Inspector For offending and insulting an officer of the law. And causing an affray.

Giovanni What affray? What insults? You've got it wrong. I was merely making the point to my wife that the police aren't all the same and that the previous sergeant, the other one, took the view that *you* were all brainless servants of... of... of...

Inspector Who's you? Me? The police?

Antonia Yes. No. I dunno. Giovanni.

Giovanni I said, no *he* said, you, meaning them, the other police — the carabinieri.

Antonia No!

Giovanni *Not* the carabinieri. Naturally. Course not. I mean, would he?

Inspector Well, as his lot probably are brainless servants to the public. And quite right. Let him go. You be careful in future.

Giovanni I will be. Don't worry.

Inspector Where was I?

The INSPECTOR *approaches sofa to finish search.*

Antonia Moan. Go on moan.

Margherita Aaaoouu.

Antonia Louder.

Margherita AAAAAOOOOOOUUUIIII.

Inspector My God. What's that? What's the matter with her?

Antonia Can't you tell?

Inspector Not really.

Antonia She's in labour, poor soul.

Giovanni Premature birth. Five months, at least.

Antonia She had a trauma earlier when the police wanted to check out her stomach.

Inspector Check out her stomach?

Giovanni That's right. To see if she was hiding rice and spaghetti packets up there. I ask you! But of course she's just a working woman without any influence. She's not Pirelli's wife who could cause a lot of trouble for you. So go ahead. How about an all round strip search —

Margherita Aaaooouuu!

Giovanni You see? Go on, turn the place over, wreck everything, finger-print the place, turn everything out, the wife's undies, why not? Turn the whole place upside down. X-ray the place.

Inspector Oi. Cut it out! This incitement.

Antonia Yes. Cut it out. You're overdoing it.

Margherita Aaaoooouuu!

Antonia And don't you overdo it, either.

Inspector Have you called an ambulance?

Giovanni An ambulance?

Inspector Well, that's the minimum facility you need to get her to hospital. In any case she might die on you. And if it's premature, she might lose the child.

Giovanni He's right. I told you we should have called an ambulance.

Antonia Yeah, and I told you she hasn't got a bed booked. She'll be driving round every hospital in town. She'll kick the bucket on the road.

Siren.

Inspector There's the ambulance we called for that woman who felt sick upstairs.

Antonia Not Rosa? From the fifth floor?

Inspector I don't know. This is a real emergency. Come on, let's carry her down.

Antonia Don't touch her. She's too nervous. She won't go.

Margherita No, I don't want to go to hospital!

Antonia See, she doesn't want to go.

Margherita I want my husband.

Antonia She wants her husband.

Margherita Luigi.

Antonia Her husband, Luigi.

Margherita Luigi, Luigi.

Antonia You see. She wants her husband. Who wouldn't? And him on nights. We can't take the responsibility without her husband's consent.

Giovanni Now that's true. We can't.

Inspector Who can't. Will you take the responsibility when she dies on you?

Antonia Why? What difference does it make at the hospital?

Inspector It'd be negligence. Their responsibility. You could sue.

Giovanni But it's premature.

Margherita Yes, yes, I'm premature. Aaaaoooui!

Antonia And with the jolting of the ambulance, she'll give birth. It can't survive in the back of an ambulance.

Inspector You've clearly no notion of the advances of modern medicine. You must have heard of oxygen tents.

Giovanni What's a five month premature baby going to do with an oxygen tent? Camp?

Inspector In extreme cases, they can even transplant them.

Giovanni and Antonia Transplants?!

Inspector Yes. Easy as pie. They perform a caesarian operation...

Margherita Aaaaaooooouuu!

Antonia Now look what you've done.

Inspector ...and transfer the whole shebang, baby, placenta, the lot to another woman who's had another caesarian.

Giovanni Another mother?

Inspector Exactly. Then they sew everyone up and Bob's your uncle. Five months later out it pops safe and sound and fit as a fiddle, yelling fit to bust.

Antonia Sounds very dodgy to me.

Giovanni A baby born twice. A child of two mothers.

Margherita No! I don't want to! Aaaaooooouuuu!

Antonia She's right, poor girl. I'd never give my baby for another woman to deliver.

Margherita No I don't want to. Ugh. No, no.

Antonia See? She doesn't want to. We can't cart her off if she doesn't want to go.

Inspector I can. On the grounds of diminished responsibility due to extreme pain. Never let it be said the carabinieri are unhelpful or turn their back on suffering.

Antonia I protest. This is out and out violence. First they frisk us, then they wreck the place, then they handcuff us, now they want to load us on to ambulances without a by-your-leave. If they won't let us live as we want, at least let us die where we choose.

Inspector No. You can't die where you choose.

Giovanni I knew there'd be a law against it.

Inspector Watch yourself.

Antonia Leave off. Giovanni, it's no good, let's get her down.

Inspector I'll get the stretcher.

Antonia No she'll walk. She's got enough troubles. You can walk, can't you?

Margherita (*Getting up.*) Yes, yes. (*Lying down quick.*) No, no. It's slipping.

Antonia Damn it. Would you mind getting out a minute. My friend is a little bit naked and I've got to dress her.

Inspector Right. All out.

The men exit.

Antonia Quick, pull up your bags! Typical, isn't it? You need a cop they're nowhere in sight. Then when you don't want them they're swarming all over the place. It's the same with the ambulance. I dunno.

Margherita I'm scared stiff. I knew it was going to end like this. What's going to happen when I get to the hospital and they find out I'm pregnant with shopping?

Antonia Nothing'll happen. We're not going to the hospital.

Margherita You're right. We're going to prison.

Antonia Oh stop whining. Pessimist. When we get into the ambulance we'll talk to the driver. They're good blokes. They'll help us.

Margherita And if they don't. If they drive straight round to the nearest nick?

Antonia Oh, cut it out. They won't. They wouldn't dare.

Margherita It's slipping. Another bag. It's coming out.

Antonia Hang on to it! Ooo, you're such a pain.

Margherita Don't shove! You'll bust something. (*They freeze.*) Oh! You've bust something.

Olives shower down from a split bag.

Antonia What?

Margherita A bag of olives has split and it's leaking all over me.

Antonia You are a nuisance!

Re-enter men.

Giovanni What's going on, now?

Margherita It's coming out, it's all coming out!

Giovanni The baby's coming already. Don't panic. Inspector, quick, help me carry her!

Inspector (*Behind him.*) I'm here.

Giovanni Oh.

Inspector Stand aside, you haven't got the training.

Antonia Now keep her horizontal, for God's sake.

Giovanni Might it come shooting out?

Inspector She's dripping.

Antonia Yes, she's broken water.

Giovanni Is that good?

Inspector It means she's near her time! Hurry.

Antonia All right, calm down. Gently with her.

Margherita Very gently! It's coming — Oooo it's coming!

Antonia Hang on. Wrap her in this blanket. (*Wraps her in blanket.*) Gently, Inspector, please.

Giovanni I'll get my coat and come too.

Antonia No. You stay here. This is women's business. You mop the floor.

Giovanni Right. Right. I'll mop the floor. Don't worry about a thing. (*They've gone.*) What a bleeding riot! Poor old Luigi'll get back knackered from the night shift and find himself a dad. He'll have a heart attack. When he finds out his child's been transplanted to another woman, he'll have a counter-attack. I'll have to break it to him gently. A really roundabout way. I'll start with the Pope. That's roundabout enough. (*Mopping.*) Blimey, all this water. (*He's now crawling on all fours, mopping up the floor with the rag.*) Blimey, all this water! But, what a strange smell, like vinegar... yeah, sort of brine, that's it. I'll be dammed, I didn't know that before being born we spent nine months in brine?! Hello?... what's this now? An olive? Olives and brine? I can't believe it! No, I must be crazy. Olives don't come into it! Oh, look, there, another one! Two olives? If it wasn't for their rather uncertain origin, I'd eat them... I'm so hungry! I almost feel like making myself some millet soup. It might even be good. I'll stick in two stock-cubes... a head of onion.. (*He opens the fridge.*) What's my welding equipment doing here? I've told her not to use it to light the gas. (*He lights gas with it.*)

Luigi Can I come in? Anybody home?

Giovanni Hello, Luigi. Why aren't you at work?

Luigi (*Gasps.*) This'll kill you.

Giovanni There's a Cuban?

Luigi (*Gasps.*) This'll kill you!!

Giovanni A Cuban wants to kill me?!!

Luigi Something's happened. We all got to the factory gates this morning... This'll kill you — tell you in a minute... first, you seen the wife? I've been home, doors wide open, nobody there.

Giovanni Ah. That's because she was here.

Luigi Oh good.

Giovanni But she's popped out with Antonia. Ten minutes ago.

Luigi Oh. Where to? And what to do?

Giovanni You know. Women's things.

Luigi What women's things?

Giovanni You know. Women's business. None of our business.

Luigi What do you mean it's none of our business? It's some of my business.

Giovanni Oh it is, is it? Suddenly, all of a sudden. Then how come you never booked a bed when you should have?

Luigi Booked a bed? What for?

Giovanni What for? What for? Dear oh dear oh me. That's it. That's men all over. We give them the pay packet, 'You'll have to manage on that,' insist on the conjugal rights, get pregnant, 'Take the pill,' and nightmares, if you're a Catholic, featuring the Pope. Then it's the nappies and the nurseries...

Luigi Er. Giovanni. What are you talking about?

Giovanni I'm saying we exploit them as surely as we are exploited by our boss!

Luigi Oh, that's what you're saying? But what has this to do with Margherita being out, leaving the door wide open, without so much as a little note and disappearing just like that?

Giovanni Why should she leave a note when she expects you to be at work until breakfast time? Tell me that? And why aren't you at work?

Luigi The train was held up.

Giovanni Broken down!

Luigi No. We held it up.

Giovanni I know there's always breakdowns on that — You what?

Luigi Well, they put the season tickets up by thirty per cent!

Giovanni How can you stop a train?

Luigi It's easy. You just pull the alarm. There's me, Tonino, Marco we got down on to the tracks and held up all the other trains. You should have been there. Middle of nowhere.

Giovanni What other trains?

Luigi All of them. Even the inter-city and the Paris Express. (*Eats olive.*)

Giovanni Oh, brilliant. Why couldn't I have thought of that? Ticket prices go up, so the entire European railway network has to be disrupted. Marvellous! Don't you realise these wild man guerrilla tactics disrupting industry play right into the hands of the reactionaries?

Luigi Quite right. That's what I told the others. Totally senseless. Not worth trying to reduce the fares. We've got to abolish them completely.

Giovanni No fares at all!?

Luigi Just what I said. The firm ought to pay. And they ought to pay us from the time we leave home. We're not sight-seeing when we're getting to work, we're getting to work.

Giovanni What are you babbling about? I know. You've been talking to a lot of maniac provocateurs, infiltrators and police agents.

Luigi What Tonino? Marco? Police agents? No. I thought them up myself. It wasn't difficult, you know. What is quite clear is that it's no good working people waiting for the government to do something, the union's intervention and a good word from your party. We have to stop expecting a white paper from the government and a strongly worded declaration of intent from the union every time we want to turn round and have a piss! If we don't do things for ourselves, then no one will.

Giovanni You haven't been talking to a copper without a moustache?

Luigi You what?

Giovanni That extremist copper that goes round trying to incite supermarket riots.

Luigi Never heard of him. (*Tasting dog food.*) Here. Nice this. What is it?

Giovanni Have you been eating that?

Luigi Yes, it's not bad. Sorry. Were you saving it?

Giovanni You had it without lemon?

Luigi Should I put some lemon on it?

Giovanni I don't know. Are you sure it tastes all right?

Luigi Yeah. Lovely.

Giovanni Let me taste.

Luigi All right, innit?

Giovanni Not bad. Want to start on this one? (*Passing other tin.*)

Luigi Certainly. What is it?

Giovanni A sort of pâté for rich cats and dogs.

Luigi Pâté for cats and dogs! Are you barmy?

Giovanni No. A gourmet. Here. Taste this. (*Puts soup saucepan on the table.*)

Luigi What is it?

Giovanni Speciality of mine: millet soup garnished with frozen rabbits' heads.

Luigi Frozen?

Giovanni That's so they won't rot. Speciality de la maison.

Luigi The millet's a bit underdone.

Giovanni That's the secret of the recipe. Underdone millet, medium-done rabbits' heads. Oi. Who's gone and eaten that olive?

Luigi What olive? Oh, that olive. Shouldn't I have?

Giovanni No, you shouldn't have. It was your wife's olive. Blimey, he even nicks the food from his baby's mouth.

Luigi My wife's olive. The baby's mouth. Here. What are you talking about?

Giovanni Don't you know nothing? You heard of natural child birth, the rhythm method? You have heard of biology?

Luigi No. Not a lot.

Giovanni When you're born, there's all this brine sort of stuff, dribbling about, see? Wait a minute. I'll start from the beginning. Right. Take it step by step. Now there's Pope Paul, right, nagging all the women and scaring the pants off them with pregnancy —

Luigi The Pope's pregnant?

Giovanni Not him. Your wife. I'm talking about your wife.

Luigi Has my wife been seeing the Pope?

Giovanni I see, pretend you don't know.

Luigi No, I don't know! What's all this about the Pope?

Giovanni You know what the Pope says in your wife's dreams?

Luigi I've no idea.

Giovanni 'Don't take the pill,' my son.

Luigi But she doesn't take the pill.

Giovanni So you *do* know.

Luigi Know what?

Giovanni She doesn't take the pill.

Luigi I just told you.

Giovanni Who's told you?

Luigi Nobody's told me. I know already. No point in the pill. She can't have kids, something wrong with the waterworks.

Giovanni Nothing at all wrong with her waterworks, mate. I've just had to mop it all up.

Luigi You've mopped up my wife's waterworks?!

Giovanni Well, not exactly water, more like brine. And a few olives. You've just eaten one.

Luigi You've lost me. Can we go back to the Pope?

Giovanni No thanks. Look, Margherita had herself all bandaged up and Antonia made her undo it and, wallop, out it popped.

Luigi My Margherita?

Giovanni Now they've gone off to hospital in an ambulance as she was about to give birth in here.

Luigi Here?

Giovanni No there. (*Pointing to couch.*)

Luigi Don't piss about. Where's my wife?

Giovanni Told you, in hospital.

Luigi Which hospital?

Giovanni Who knows. If you had booked it, we'd know, wouldn't we? As it is the poor little bleeder will probably be born in the ambulance on the way there with all them olives.

Luigi Will you leave the olives out of this! Tell me which hospital she's gone to.

Giovanni It's the gynaecological clinic.

Luigi Do you mean the baby clinic?

Giovanni Where they transplant the premature baby from one belly to another.

Luigi Transplants?

Giovanni Yeah?

Luigi Baby transplants??

Giovanni Oh. You've heard of it.

Luigi No.

Giovanni That's it. It's obvious you're totally ignorant of modern techniques of premature delivery.

Luigi Yes, I am.

Giovanni They get a baby tent, blow it up, like, with oxygen, then they put the mothers under... No, it's the fathers... No, I mean the kid, then they take the other mother after she's had her caesarian, fully automatic...

Luigi Cut it out will you!

Giovanni Exactly what they do!!

Luigi I don't give a monkey's about no baby tent, transplant or fully automatic caesarian. I want to know where this gynaecology place is. Where's the phone book?

Giovanni I haven't got one.

Luigi Why not?

Giovanni No phone.

Luigi I'm going down the bar. They've got one.

Giovanni Hold it. Niguarda! Niguarda clinic!

Luigi Niguarda. Blimey, that's the other side of town. Why have they taken her that far?

Giovanni I told you. It's where they've developed this special technique. The transplant. They get the other woman. The first one prepared to take the child off the donor, a friend perhaps, and they take her into the hospital — some dozy old cow who's loony enough to contemplate the idea in the first place. Anyway they get this woman — My wife! She's so stupid she'll say yes straight away. Come on we've got to make this phone call. Luigi, I'm sorry to say this, but I can't give my permission.

Luigi Who's asking?

Giovanni But I'm the next of kin.

Luigi Not to me you ain't.

Giovanni I am the husband.

Luigi No, no, no. You're the husband to the second mother. I'm the husband to the first mother.

Giovanni But the transplanted mother is mine!

Luigi I don't give a monkey's. I'm giving my permission and that's that.

Giovanni Are you sure?

Luigi No.

Giovanni I tell you if you go ahead with this, I'll pack her off to live with you.

Luigi She already does.

Giovanni *My wife*, I mean. You can keep her. If she's going to feed your kid, you can keep me too.

Luigi Why you too?

Giovanni I'm the other father, ain't I?

Luigi Yeah, but I'm the first father.

Giovanni Yeah, but I'm the first other other father.

They exit ad libbing.

END OF ACT ONE

ACT II

Antonia (*Off.*) Giovanni? Giovanni? Can I borrow your spanner? (*Enters.*) Thank God. He's not in. Blimey, look at the time we've been gone for more than four hours. Come on Margherita, come in. He must have already gone to work, he can't even have had a kip yet poor old sod. Y'know Ma... (*Opens door.*) You dozy cow.

Margherita Is he in?

Antonia No he's not. Come in.

Margherita It's all your fault. You never listen to me. Look at the mess we're in.

Antonia Oh, stop whining. Blimey what a pain. We haven't been caught out yet. The ambulance men were great.

Margherita Yes, they were.

Antonia And you were worried about it! You've got to trust people. Who's nicked the butter? (*Looking in fridge.*) Oh, here it is. I'll make some soup. Hello, what's this? (*Tastes.*) Oh, Giovanni. He's made some soup. Ohh. Can your Luigi look after himself when you're not around? Mmmm nice aroma. Oh millet! Very experimental. Wonder what else he's put in it... Rabbits' heads!!! You can't even tell a lie without him swallowing it. I'll make some proper soup. You should hear the fuss when I put something in front of him. Well, I'll show him. Rabbits' heads with raspberry yoghurt. Rabbits' heads with custard. Rabbits' heads with chicken liver and brown sauce. It'll be curried rabbits' heads from now on. Here you've gone all green Margherita.

Margherita Listen, if you're only making the soup for me, don't bother.

Antonia Oh go on.

Margherita I'm not hungry suddenly. My stomach is all knotted up.

Antonia This'll unknot it for you. You shouldn't be so nervous. Most people are decent underneath. Not everybody, of course. But people like us. Working people having a job making ends meet. People like that are on our side, as long as you show them you won't let the bosses kick you in the teeth, that you're prepared to fight for your rights, and don't wait for St Peter to leave his pearly gates and come down and do it all for you. I remember when I worked at the biscuit factory. What a bloody job. But it was a living. Then suddenly the owners decided to 'rationalise' the place, as they call it, because profits were down. In fact, they were only kicking us out because they were planning to close it completely. So we occupied the place. Three hundred of us. Then we started to run the place, we formed a co-operative. Especially the union leaders. 'It's a losing battle, brothers,' they told us. But do you know what? All of us put every penny we could spare into the factory. Some people put their savings in and one bloke even sold his flat. All of us pawned silver and stuff that we never saw again. Sheets and blankets even. That's how we got our first bag of flour. We went round the shops ourselves with the biscuits and sold them at the factory gates. Plenty of people bought biscuits they didn't need, just to help us out. And to show solidarity. Then when things got bad for us, thousands of workers collected money for us. I'll never forget when they brought the money in. We were all kneading the dough as usual and they put the money on the table. All wrapped up in a big dishcloth — a great big pile, and all the women started to cry like rain into the dough. Nobody moved and nobody spoke. We just went on mixing tears and dough for biscuits. What are you crying for now?

Margherita It's the story...

Antonia Well what about it?

Margherita It's so moving. I'm dripping everywhere.

Antonia Yeah, well, before we all get drowned, just you have a think about what I'm saying. It's not just a fairy story, you know. It ain't got a happy ending.

Margherita What happened?

Antonia The CP moved in, didn't they? 'You can't last out,' they said. So they persuaded us to negotiate with the management. That was the end of it. Two months later the factory closed down. Another 300 jobs up the spout. The fights I had with Giovanni about that. I nearly left him. Reformist git. Anyway, enough of all that. What are you doing?

Margherita Unloading.

She is taking the shopping off.

Antonia Not here. We'll stash the stuff in dad's allotment shed. It's only round the corner. The gear'll be safe there. I'll make myself a big belly, too. In two or three trips we'll be done.

Margherita No. No. No, no, no, no. I'm dead tired and I'm not going on. I'm leaving the lot here. I don't want any of it.

Antonia You dozy cow.

Margherita I see, I'm a dozy cow, am I? Well, you with all your bright ideas can work out what I'm going to tell my old man when he discovers that I'm not pregnant after all.

Antonia That's simple. We'll tell him you had a phantom pregnancy.

Margherita What's that?

Antonia Happens all the time. A woman thinks she's pregnant, her belly swells up and then, when the baby's about to come out, she just gives birth to a lot of wind.

Margherita That's not very nice. How could that happen to me?

Antonia Simple. Because of the Pope keeping coming into your dreams and telling you: 'Havea da child, my childa.' And you made a child, only it was a lot of hot air. Like the Pope.

Margherita Antonia! How can you drag the Pope into this business?

Antonia Well, he's always dragging us into his business, isn't he? Do this, do that, all you wops keep off my grass. Why can't women be priests? You could be a good priest Margherita. You're a good listener.

Margherita Do you think so?

Antonia Right, I'm ready. I'll be back in ten minutes. Keep an eye on the soup.

Margherita Why can't we forget the belly business and take the shopping bags over in one trip?

Antonia And what will you do when the law stops you? Now watch the gas and if it goes out light it with that thing.

Margherita What's that?

Antonia It's Giovanni's welder. Light it like this. (ANTONIA *shows her.*)

Margherita Doesn't it get red hot?

Antonia No. It's not iron. It's some stuff called antimony and it gets really hot without ever glowing. So don't touch it. Now let's see if the coast's clear.

They go to the window.

Margherita That's Maria.

Antonia From the third floor.

Margherita She's pregnant, too.

Antonia The men'll be at it soon.

Margherita What, pregnant?!

Antonia No hunchbacks. Right. I'm off. Don't forget this. (*Starts for the door.*)

Margherita I've changed my mind. I'm coming with you. (*Loads up.*)

Antonia Good. You've been thinking about my biscuit factory.

Margherita Yes. But I'm willing to co-operate.

Antonia You know, all this out here reminds me of my baby.

Margherita Your baby?

Antonia Nearly a man now. Couldn't wait to get out and get a job. He got out alright, but he's still waiting for a job.

Margherita What's a job? I've forgotten what it was when you could get one.

Antonia Yeah, mind you, they won't break his spirit. He'll just get cross. If they get on the wrong side of him they'll know what for. Right! Are you ready?

Both exit.

The street. LUIGI *enters, walking determinedly, followed by the exhausted* GIOVANNI.

Giovanni Luigi, I'm knackered. (*He sits.*) If they say on the phone that your wife isn't at their hospital, do we have to check it out? Don't you trust them?

Luigi Would you? With baby transplants?

Giovanni Now you mention it, no. But my feet are killing me.

LUIGI *looks skyward.*

Luigi Oh no.

Giovanni What?

Luigi Rain.

Giovanni Shit.

Luigi Bloody government.

Giovanni Look, let's give up. I'm getting off to work. I've lost time already.

Luigi (*Remembering*.) Oh yeah. I wanted to tell you something about that. About the firm.

Giovanni (*Loud crash*.) What's that? Hold it. Wait a minute. Look at that!

Luigi Jesus. What a mess.

Giovanni It's a juggernaut.

Luigi Must have skidded and jack-knifed.

Giovanni Someone better watch all them sacks or someone's liable to nick them.

Enter SERGEANT *from right*.

Sergeant All right. Keep calm. Don't panic. Stand back. It's all right. No one's hurt. Don't panic. (*Exit left*.)

Luigi Who's panicking?

Giovanni Hello. Keep meeting, him and me.

Luigi Know him?

Giovanni Good mates. I can't work him out. He's either a Maoist or an agent provocateur...

Luigi Agent provocateur. Definitely.

Giovanni Just what I said.

Enter SERGEANT.

Sergeant Stand back, there. That's dangerous stuff. It could blow any time.

Giovanni That won't blow. That's caustic soda. That's what it says on the lorry.

Sergeant Yes. Well. That's what it says on the outside. But appearances can be deceiving.

Giovanni You don't trust anything do you?

Sergeant I know you, don't I?

Giovanni Yeah. You was round my house.

Sergeant Oh yeah. Anyway, things aren't always what they seem.

Giovanni Blimey, mate. We're talking about clearly labelled International Road transport. We're talking about Common Market regulations! We're talking about border certificates in triplicate! And I'm talking about something else. When this rain gets into that soda it's going to smoulder into a right smelly old pudding. So someone ought to get that stuff out of the rain.

Sergeant You're right. How we going to do that?

LUIGI *taps* GIOVANNI *'s shoulder*.

Giovanni Shouldn't be too much of a problem.

Luigi Giovanni.

Giovanni Well, let's have a look.

Luigi Giovanni.

Giovanni Best thing is form a chain...

Luigi Giovanni.

Giovanni ...mobilise those fellows over there, get all the stuff back over there.

Sergeant Very good idea. I'll get them going, you man this area. Brilliant idea. (*Goes off left.*) Oi! You lot! Give us a hand here.

Giovanni Fuck me and my big ideas.

Luigi You'll never listen and never learn, will ya?

SERGEANT *re-enters.*

Sergeant (*Organising.*) OK, spread out. Pass them along. That's the way!

Sacks are thrown from left to LUIGI *to* GIOVANNI *and off right.*

Giovanni See that? You ask for help and you've got it. You shouldn't be such a pessimist. Look at that. All mucking in.

Sergeant I never said people weren't generous.

Giovanni No, but you're still a mistrustful old berk. I had a boss once like you. He couldn't trust anyone except this mangy old dog of his. He loved this dog and he decided to buy him a deaf-aid.

Luigi A deaf-aid?

Giovanni That's right.

Luigi For a dog?

Giovanni That's right. So he bought this deaf-aid and he strapped the battery to the dog's belly.

Luigi So what happened?

Giovanni The first time the dog cocked his leg to have a piss, he pissed on the battery and electrocuted himself to death.

They laugh. SERGEANT *looks puzzled.*

Sergeant There's a moral to that story. Can't think what.

Luigi Where's the drivers?

Giovanni Gone for help?

Sergeant No, done a bunk.

Giovanni Why?

Sergeant Let's have a look.

They all poke a finger into the neck of a sack and taste the contents.

Sergeant Sugar.

Luigi Flour.

Giovanni Rice! Someone's made a mistake with the labelling.

Luigi Fancy that.

Sergeant Just as I thought. It's containered at the depot and the seals aren't broken till they get there. They're flogging it round Europe. You get better prices in Switzerland. Just a bit of funny book-keeping, a few forged papers and no one's the wiser.

Luigi Unless they happen to turn over on the road. They're telling the truth for once when they talk about shortages. They're running it all out of the country. No wonder there's a shortage.

Giovanni Shortage? Shortage? What about the butter mountain? The Beaujolais lake? The Leaning Tower of Pizza? That's not shortage. That's excessage.

Sergeant You clearly don't understand the working of your Common Market.

Giovanni I certainly don't. Fill me in, *do*.

Sergeant It's to do with the Greek and Portuguese economy.

Giovanni They're not in the Common Market.

Sergeant Exactly. But they will be and then you need a strong Deutsch Mark.

Luigi O yeah?

Sergeant Course. Your German economy is dependent on the car industry, but hardly anybody can afford them dirty great German Mercedes and BMWs.

Luigi So?

Sergeant Simple. You pay your French farmer dirty great subsidies to pay for the dirty great German cars.

Giovanni You've lost me.

Luigi It's simple. It's like the Irish pigs.

Giovanni Course it is.

Luigi They keep driving them backwards and forwards over the border of Northern Ireland picking up Common Market subsidies every time. They call it 'take your pick, every trip'.

Sergeant That's it. See? Simple.

Luigi Only thing is the British Army get annoyed. Every time the pigs stampede they get trampled underfoot.

Sergeant Take this lorry, for instance. You drive all over Europe and every time you cross a border you pick up your subsidies. *And* you save labour costs because you never have to unload it.

Giovanni You'll have to take action.

Sergeant Oh, I will! Most definitely.

Giovanni What's the matter now?

Sergeant Do you want to know what'll happen from here? I shall write a full report, a model of brevity and procedure, the result of which charges will be laid. A brief item on News at Ten will allude to a brilliant police operation where contraband has been seized and men are sought. Duly alerted by the said item the industrialists will take a quick fortuitous trip over the border. Having laid my evidence before the judge, he will, with a pained expression, because it's a bit like welching on your own kind, sentence them to four months. The industrialists will hear about this whilst sunning themselves on the beaches of St Tropez and will immediately appeal to the President who will commute the sentence to a stiff fine.

Giovanni And that's the end of it?

Sergeant By no means. They'll appeal the stiff fine and get off with a stiff talking to.

Luigi You what?

Sergeant And they get their sugar, rice and flour back. (*Looks off left.*) Oi! Where are you going with them bags? (*Exits.*)

Giovanni It's criminal, that's what it is.

Luigi Mr Gullible. (*Making a decision.*) Grab a bag.

Giovanni What for?

Luigi We're going to whip a couple.

Giovanni Oh yeah?

Luigi Oh yeah!

Giovanni Are you out of your mind? Are you descending to the level of that rabble over there?

Luigi That's right. That rabble over there! Blimey, what is all this middle-class shit? You sound like a Social Democrat — alright, not that bad.

Giovanni I don't steal what isn't mine.

Luigi Well you're all right, because it is yours. So steal away. Blimey, do I have to spell it out to you? Who produces it? Who sows it? Who reaps it? Who processes it and packs it? Who cooks it and eats it?

Giovanni Luigi. You're looking after Number One. It's a slippery slope you're on. You won't have a principled bone left in your body soon. That's just the excuse they want.

Luigi Who?

Giovanni The military? That's who! They only have to call this a breakdown in law and order and they can roll out the troops and the tanks, suspend the constitution, and before you can say fettuccine, we have fascism.

Luigi Oh? What do you suggest then?

Giovanni Legal action through the unions.

Luigi Oh, terrific.

Giovanni Against the unions are we? All right. All right. Who mobilised the entire workforce at Fiat's to strike in the dinner hour?

Luigi Who organised the women today? Not the unions. The women rioted because they can't take any more. See these hands? They want what's theirs. But your union leaders and your precious party tie them behind our backs. And that's when the army take over. Not when you're on the offensive, but when you're being led up the garden. No. What we want's leadership, mate. Oh, by the way, that reminds me, I was going to tell you about the firm.

Giovanni Yes?

Luigi What's the union doing about that?

Giovanni Doing about what?

INSPECTOR *approaches unobserved.*

Inspector What's going on here?

Luigi Do you mind not interrupting?

Inspector What's going on?

Luigi Bugger off. (*Seeing* INSPECTOR.) Oh!

Luigi We're slogging away here for the balance of payments.

Giovanni Blimey, don't he look like the other one?

Luigi You're right. The one without the moustache.

Inspector What you on about?

Luigi Forget it.

Inspector What are you doing holding them bags?

Luigi These?

Inspector I don't see any other type of bags littering the place.

Luigi Oh. We're moving them to a safe place.

Inspector Where did they come from?

Luigi Fell off the back of a lorry.

Inspector I bet.

Giovanni Trying to be helpful, that's all.

Inspector Yeah. Helping yourself.

Giovanni Ask the sergeant. He said to move them. He asked us to.

Inspector Which sergeant?

Giovanni Over there.

INSPECTOR *pulls pistol and* LUIGI *and* GIOVANNI *shoot their hands up.*

Inspector Don't you move a muscle. You'll get shot. (*Off left.*)

Luigi Now we'll go and get shot.

Giovanni Yeah. The police have a funny habit of accidentally shooting people on purpose.

Luigi Bastard.

Giovanni Mind you, he's all right. He's the one who helped your wife into the ambulance with the olives.

Luigi Stuff the olives. (*Remembering.*) Oh yeah. The firm. I've been trying to tell you. We've been made redundant.

Giovanni We haven't. Nobody told me.

Luigi We have.

Luigi Everyone in the night shift got a dear John from the management. You'll get yours. They're closing down and moving somewhere else.

Giovanni We're supposed to have a full order book.

Luigi They're going to move somewhere where the labour is cheaper.

Giovanni Labour doesn't come any cheaper than us!

Luigi It does now.

GIOVANNI *stands thinking, hands up. Then dropping them suddenly.*

Giovanni That's it. I'm finished. Pass me my bag.

Luigi You can't do that.

Giovanni Who can't? It's ours, ain't it?

They start to exit right with bags. INSPECTOR *enters left.*

Inspector Oi. Freeze!

Pause.

Giovanni Inspector. Catch.

GIOVANNI *throws bag high in the air.* LUIGI *throws a bag to* GIOVANNI *and grabs another.*

Luigi Run! — (*Exit pursued by* INSPECTOR.)

Another part of town. GIOVANNI *cycles on with* LUIGI *and two sacks on the crossbar.*

Giovanni Another hundred yards and we've made it.

LUIGI *falls off.*

Stop mucking about.

Luigi I still think you shouldn't have nicked the bike.

Giovanni I haven't nicked it. I told you. I've liberated it.

Luigi Liberated? What if it belongs to a poor blind granny?

Giovanni What's a poor blind granny doing on a bike?

Luigi Forty miles an hour.

Giovanni Blimey, a police van. Outside my house.

Luigi Here, look, those two women. Isn't that your old lady?

Giovanni No. Looks like yours though.

Luigi They're going into your block. That one's pregnant.

Giovanni You're right. No look. They're both pregnant.

Luigi Oh yes. It can't be them. It must be two others completely.

Giovanni Shit. Look.

Luigi What. What?

Giovanni That bleeding copper has been following us. With half the town doing all the nicking why does he have to pick on us?

Luigi He knows where you live. That's why. He'll be waiting round your house for when you get there.

Giovanni You're right. All right, we'll go round your house. He won't think of that.

They exit right. After a moment the INSPECTOR *puffs across the stage still carrying his bag. Blackout.*

ANTONIA's *house.* ANTONIA *and* MARGHERITA *are discovered hanging shopping round their necks and buttoning their coats over it.*

Antonia Come on Margherita. Let's load up. This is the last trip.

Margherita Thank goodness. Load up. Unload. Load up. Unload. I feel like a lorry.

Antonia Stop moaning.

Margherita Look, enough salad to last a month.

Antonia Yes, I went a bit mad on the salad. I hope we don't get caught this trip. I'd hate to get frisked with a belly full of celery.

Margherita You've got a point there.

ANTONIA *at the gas stove.*

Antonia Oh shit. The soup hasn't cooked. They've cut the gas off. It'll be the electricity next. Bloody bastards.

Knock, knock.

Antonia Who is it?

Inspector (*Off.*) I've a message from your husband.

Antonia Oh my God, something happened! (*Starts to the door.*)

Margherita Antonia! The salad!

Antonia Stuff it! (*They hastily conceal bags of salad.*) Can you wait? I'm only half-naked.

INSPECTOR *enters carrying bag of flour.*

Inspector Stop. Turn round. Don't touch a thing. Caught red-handed. You can't fool me with those bellies of yours.

Antonia What you on about?

Margherita Here we go. I knew it. Aaaaoouuu!

Inspector Madam, congratulations. I'm happy to see you didn't lose your child. (*To* ANTONIA.) And to you too, madam. In five hours you've made love, got pregnant and appear to be about in the ninth month of your confinement! It's a miracle.

Antonia You better watch it cos my husband will...

Inspector Will what?

Antonia Be home soon.

Inspector Right, open up. Let's have it.

Antonia Have what?

Inspector Persistent little jailbird, aren't we? Don't think I haven't worked out the *modus operandi* with the belly. There was a point today when I thought that I was going mad. Every single woman — from nymphets of eight to great grandmothers of eighty-eight — pregnant!

Antonia Well, exactly. There you are. That explains it. Doesn't it. (*Improvising.*) Surely you have heard of the Feast of St Evlalia.

Inspector I can't say I have and what's that to the point?

Antonia Yes. St Evlalia, the patron saint of fertility.

Inspector St Evlalia? Fertility? What's all this fertility? St Evlalia...

Antonia Er.

Margherita St Evlalia, the woman who was barren until she was sixty and then was miraculously blessed with a child by our Lord.

Inspector Sixty years old?

Antonia Yes. Her old man was eighty. Not up on our saints are we? Mind you, he did die. To celebrate this miracle the women in this area go about with fake stomachs.

Inspector What a touching tradition. And the tradition gives you *carte blanche* to loot supermarkets, what's more. Amazing, the power of religion in this day and age. Right, that's enough nefarious twaddle. Open up.

Antonia Oh yes, have the clothes off our backs! That's it! Go ahead! If you lay one finger on our bellies a terrible thing will happen to you.

Inspector Like what?

Antonia Yes...

Margherita The curse of St Evlalia.

Antonia Yeah, that.

Inspector What curse?

Antonia The same curse that befell her old man. When he first saw her with child. 'You pregnant? Do us a favour! Show us what you've got under there! And if you *are* pregnant I'll do you in because I can't be the father, that's for certain.' So St Evlalia exposed herself, so to speak, and out poured a cascade of roses.

Inspector What a lovely little story.

Antonia Wait for it. I haven't finished yet. Soon after a heavy darkness fell on his eyes. 'I can't see,' he shouted, 'I'm going blind.' And then a minute later, 'I am blind!' Then St Evlalia said, 'See what God does to unbelievers.'

Inspector This gets better and better.

Margherita Yes, it does.

Antonia Really?

Margherita Of course!!

Antonia Well, alright then. And then there was a third miracle. From out of the masses of roses pops a little child ten months old already. Speaking perfect Italian with a perfect set of teeth. 'Papa,' he says, 'the Lord forgives you.' Then he touches the old man, who was quite surprised, on the head, who falls down dead there and then. But peacefully.

Inspector You finished? Right, come on, let's see the roses.

Antonia Well that's enough isn't it?

Inspector Right, come on, let's see the roses.

Antonia So you're a disbeliever?

Inspector Yes. Very.

Antonia You're not afraid of the curse?

Inspector What curse? Do me a favour!

Antonia Right you've asked for it. Margherita, we'll expose ourselves together. Do the poem.

Margherita The poem?

Antonia Yeah, the poem.

Margherita *The* poem.

Antonia Yes, the exposure poem.

Margherita Oh, the exposure poem. St Evlalia, pregnant saint,
He that says that there ain't,
In your deeds no miracles,
In your words no oracles.
Make his vision dark and thick,
Make the bastard bloody sick.
St Evlalia touch his head
Make him fall down completely and utterly dead!
Antonia Right, Margherita.

They throw open their coats and reveal string bags bursting with salad.

Inspector Gor'blimey. What's all that?
Antonia Good Lord. It's salad. Fancy that.
Inspector It's salad.
Antonia You're right. Lettuce, chicory, celery, carrots, cabbage.
Margherita I've got cabbage, too. And a teensy bit of parsley.
Antonia So you have. You know that's really difficult to get...
Inspector What's going on? What's all those greens for? Why are they so hid?
Antonia They're not so hid. It's a miracle.
Inspector Oh yes? The cabbage miracle. Where's the roses?
Margherita Who can afford roses? They're very expensive.
Antonia In hard times, one makes what miracles one can. With the veg you've got handy. Anyway, miracles aren't illegal, you know.
Inspector Don't be so sure of it.
Antonia Also, there's no law that says a person can't carry a mixed salad à la carte on their belly.
Inspector Don't bank on it.
Antonia A few crudities, can't hurt.
Inspector Don't be filthy. But what does it all mean?
Antonia Mean? Mean? I've told you. To celebrate St Evlalia. We have to carry a belly around for three days on pain of some fearful, terrible... pain. You can be struck —

The lights flicker for a moment and die.

Inspector It's getting dark.
Antonia Oh really?
Inspector There's something wrong with your light.
Antonia What light? What's wrong with my light?
Inspector It's gone out. It's dark.
Antonia No it hasn't. What a funny idea! It's as light as day — oh, I see, you're a comedian. He's having us on.
Inspector No. No, it's dark.
Antonia I can see perfectly well. Can't we Margherita?
Margherita Not really, no. (ANTONIA *kicks her.*) Yes, yes. Clear as day.
Antonia Yes, we can both see — oh blessed saint he's going blind.

Margherita Oh no!

Inspector Look, don't muck about. Switch on the light, please.

Antonia Of course, but it won't help. Look. Off. On. Off. On. See?

Inspector No! See, see. No I can't see. D'you see?

Antonia Oh my God, the Lord has punished this man.

Margherita Yes he has.

Inspector Open the window. Quick.

Antonia It's open already.

Margherita He can't see it.

Antonia Come and have a look. (*Moves chair in his path.*)

Margherita Over here.

Antonia Mind the chair.

Inspector Oooooowwwww! My shin!

Antonia He's bumped into the chair. What a tragedy. Mind the broom.

Inspector What?

Antonia Never mind. (*Hits him with broom.*)

Margherita I'll get you a plaster.

Antonia Mind the drawer.

Inspector (*Crash.*) Thanks.

Margherita Sorry.

Antonia Here's the window. Here, here's the window sill. Open up. See? Isn't it light outside.

INSPECTOR *peers into the cupboard.*

Margherita It is. Definitely. There's a lot of light.

Inspector Oh no. I can't see. What's happening to me? Light a match.

Antonia I'll do better than that. I'll use my husband's blowlamp. There you are. What a bright flame!

ANTONIA *proffers the welder to the* INSPECTOR.

Inspector I can't see no flame! Let me feel.

Antonia Are you barmy? You'll burn yourself.

Inspector No. I won't burn myself. OOOOooooooWWwwwwww!!!!

Antonia What's up?

Inspector I burnt myself.

Antonia That comes of unbelieving.

Inspector Yeeeooow.

Antonia Now do you believe?

Inspector I'm blind! My eyes!

Margherita That's what we've been telling you.

Inspector Let me out, show me the door!

Margherita Over there. (*Pointing to door.*)

Antonia No over here. (*Pointing to wardrobe.*) Here it is.

INSPECTOR *bangs head in cupboard as he enters. He reels out clutching his head.*

Inspector Ouuu! My head... the pain... I'm dying... my head!

Margherita He's smashed his head I think.

Antonia It's the child, he's touched you.

Inspector I'll wring his neck. The bleeding little bastard.

Antonia Language, Inspector, language. (INSPECTOR *faints*.) Blimey, he's fainted.

Margherita Are you sure he's not dead?

Antonia No I'm not.

Margherita Is he breathing?

Antonia He is... Not. He's not! My God he's stopped breathing. His heart's stopped too.

Margherita Antonia. We've killed a policeman.

Antonia Yeah, we overdid it a bit, didn't we. Never mind. What are we going to do?

Margherita What are we going to do? You did it. Don't ask me. Include me out. Where's my keys? (*Searching her pockets*.)

Antonia Great! The solidarity!

MARGHERITA *finds keys on the table*. ANTONIA *unloads her coat and salad meanwhile*.

Margherita Here they are. Wait a minute. I've got another set in my pocket! These must be my old man's! He been here!

Antonia Don't panic. He'll be back when he realises he's left them.

Margherita Don't you see? If he's been here he must have seen Giovanni —

Antonia Not surprising. He lives here.

MARGHERITA *rushes out the front door in a panic re-entering immediately*.

Margherita No! Giovanni will have told him everything. About me being pregnant, and the ambulance and the clinic and the transplant. Everything! What can I say? Oooooahhh! Sod it, I'm not moving out of here. You'll have to tell one of your stories, I can't do them like you can. You'll have to get me out of this mess.

Antonia All right, all right. I'll think of something.

Margherita What?

Antonia I can't think what. Look at him. Miserable sod. It's all his fault.

Margherita No it's not, it's all your fault.

Antonia He shouldn't have believed me. He fell for it, you know, dozy bugger. Let's have a look.

Margherita What you up to now?

Antonia Artificial respiration. What does it look like?

Margherita You don't do it like that! You have to give him the kiss of life.

Antonia What? Kiss a copper. There are limits. And what if my old man comes in? You kiss if you want.

Margherita You must be joking. We should have some oxygen for this.

Antonia Of course. Why didn't I think? Quick, help me with Giovanni's welding gear. Look, one is oxygen the other's hydrogen. We'll stick the nozzle in his gob.

She has dragged the equipment over to the body.

Margherita Are you sure it'll work?

Antonia Of course. I've seen it on the films.

Margherita Oh well, that's all right then. It must be OK.

Antonia It's working! Look, his chest is going up and d — up and up and up! It'll go down in a second, don't worry.

Margherita I'm not worried! Who's worried? Is his belly meant to go up and d — up and up and up?

Antonia Oh dear. I think we got it wrong. It's the hydrogen! He's biting on the pipe. I can't get it out of his gob. Help me pull it out! No. Pull! Tell you what, I'll turn it off. No that's the wrong way round. That's it.

Margherita Done it.

Antonia Blimey, look at the size of him! We've got a pregnant dead copper on our hands now.

Blackout.

Street outside LUIGI *'s house.* LUIGI *and* GIOVANNI *are sitting dolefully on their sacks.*

Giovanni Oh wonderful. Aren't we a clever boy. Locked out of your own house with two tons of sugar and half the police forces in the country on our heels!

Luigi Don't look at me.

Giovanni What sort of thief loses his door key. Go on, pick the lock.

Luigi I have picked the lock.

Giovanni Kick the door down.

Luigi I can't. It's got three bolts. On the inside.

Giovanni What for?

Luigi My wife is scared shitless of thieves.

Giovanni What's she worried about? *You* can't get in and you live here!

Luigi Wait a minute. I've remembered! I left my keys on your kitchen table.

Giovanni We can't go back there!

Luigi Why not? Give us your keys. I'll go.

Giovanni That Inspector will be waiting for us.

Luigi He'll have got fed up and gone home.

Giovanni Not him. He's a bleeding terrier. They never let go.

Sound off.

Giovanni What's that?!

Luigi Calm down. Just a neighbour.

Giovanni Hide the sacks!

Mild panic for a moment.

Luigi Stand on them.

Giovanni That's it. They won't notice them. Act casual.

Enter UNDERTAKER. *Very grave. Played by the same actor who plays the* SERGEANT *and the* INSPECTOR.

Undertaker I wonder if you... What are you standing on them sacks for?

Luigi What sacks?

Undertaker Those ones. There. On the ground. Underneath your feet.

Giovanni Oh, *those* ones.

Luigi We were keeping our feet dry. Rain. See?

Undertaker Oh. Anyway, do you know a Sergio Prampolini?

Luigi Third floor. But he's away in hospital. Very ill. Goodbye.

Undertaker No he's not there no more.

Luigi He must have discharged himself.

Undertaker Er. Not really.

Luigi He must be better. That's good.

Undertaker No he's dead.

Luigi Dead? That's bad. Jesus, that's terrible!

Undertaker I know, I know, I never get used to it and I've been in the packing business for twenty years.

Giovanni Packing?

Undertaker Yes, I pack coffins.

GIOVANNI *and* LUIGI *touch wood, touching crotch.*

Giovanni Sorry mate, force of habit.

Undertaker It's all right. Everybody does it. When I look in the mirror, I do it myself.

Luigi Charming.

Undertaker Twenty years and I'm still not used to death and grief and sorrow, the weeping widows, the distraught children. Dearie me. I mean, if you're any sort of human being you never get used to it. When will the family be back?

Luigi What good will they be? They won't want the body will they?

Undertaker Well, it wasn't at the hospital so the relatives must have it and if they don't have it God knows where it is. No, the problem is what am I going to do with the coffin?

Giovanni Leave it in the hall.

Undertaker And have kids aerosoling political statements all over it? What do you take me for? Besides, I've got to get it signed for.

Giovanni What about —

Luigi We can't help, mate.

Undertaker You live here don't you?

Luigi Who me?

Undertaker Only you could sign for it, keep it till the family come back and pass it on to them.

Luigi I've only a little flat.

Undertaker It's only a little coffin.

Luigi Can't help you, mate, anyway I'm locked out. See.

Undertaker Oh well. Back to the parlour.

Luigi Giovanni. (*Tapping* GIOVANNI*'s shoulder.*)

Giovanni Er, tell you what, I'll take it off your hands.

Luigi Giovanni.

Undertaker Can I trust you?

Giovanni I live round here.

Undertaker It's a deal. Right I'll go and get it. (*Exits.*)

Luigi Giovanni, are you barmy? We've got enough to cope with apart from looking after people's coffins.

Giovanni Luigi, answer me this: how did the Vietcong get their weapons into Saigon?

Luigi I'm sorry Magnus. I'll have to pass on that one.

Giovanni In coffins!

Luigi Terrific. Thanks for that bit of socialist history. That's not going to help us get rid of the bags... Oh!!

Giovanni See?

Undertaker (*Off.*) Ready!

Giovanni I'll be the corpse. You be the widow. You can carry it with the undertaker.

Luigi I don't think widows carry coffins very often. They haven't got the legs for it. Neither have I.

Giovanni There's no answer to that.

Luigi Tell you what. I'll borrow his hat.

They start to go.

Giovanni Here. Don't he look like the one with the moustache?

Luigi No. The one without.

Giovanni Really?

Blackout.

GIOVANNI *and* ANTONIA*'s flat.*

ANTONIA *re-arranges bags and buttons coat.* SERGEANT *lies where he fell.*

Margherita Oh, sod you, Antonia. Here we are with a dead copper on our hands and you're still playing silly buggers with the salad.

Antonia What else can we do? This'll be our last trip anyway and, as for him, if he's dead he's dead and if he's alive he'll wake up soon enough and thank the Lord for getting his sight and health back and for getting pregnant.

Margherita Very funny.

Antonia Now let's hide him under the sofa.

Margherita Do we have to touch him?

Antonia No. The cupboard. I've seen it in films.

Margherita Oh well then. (*They lift him.*) Jesus he weighs a ton.

Antonia My God, my back's killing me. Get him upright. That's it. (*They drag him into the wardrobe.*) Stick a hanger in his jacket. Now hang him on the bar. There. Shut the door. Let's see if its raining.

MARGHERITA *goes to window.*

Margherita Yes. It is raining.

Antonia I'll get my wellies and a brolly.

ANTONIA *exits into bedroom.* LUIGI *enters.*

Luigi Anybody home?

Margherita No.

Luigi Eh?

Margherita Nobody's home.

Luigi You're here.

Margherita I am.

Luigi I think so.

Margherita So I am. (*Laughs.*)

Luigi What are you laughing at?

Margherita I'm getting hysterical. Where did you get that hat? Where did you get that hat?

Luigi Isn't it a lovely... Forget the hat. What about you? I've tramped half of Milan looking for you. Are you all right, love, and the baby, you haven't lost it?

Margherita Don't worry. Everything's all right.

Luigi Are you sure? Tell me everything.

Margherita Everything?

Luigi Of course!

Margherita Tell you what. Antonia is much better than me at explaining things. I'll go and get her.

Luigi All right.

Undertaker (*Off.*) Ready.

Margherita What was that noise?

Luigi What noise?

Margherita A voice.

Luigi A voice? I can explain everything.

Margherita So can I.

Luigi You can?

Margherita I'll get Antonia.

MARGHERITA *exits to bedroom.*

Luigi (*At front door.*) OK. Bring it in.

LUIGI *and* UNDERTAKER *bring coffin in.*

Margherita (*Off.*) Antonia! Come out quickly.

Giovanni (*In the coffin.*) The women are in!

Antonia Can't I even piss in peace?

Luigi She noticed my hat.

Undertaker I've got four more deliveries to make. Goodbye. I don't know, what a life. Weeping widows, distraught children. All these quick changes... (*Exits.*)

Luigi I preferred him as the Inspector.

Giovanni Yeah. Now, what are we going to tell Antonia?

Luigi I know. Lock the bedroom door, we'll stuff the sack under the sofa and stand the coffin in the cupboard.

Giovanni Good idea.

Margherita (*Off.*) Antonia, I have to talk to you.

Antonia (*Off.*) Sod it! It's all slipping out.

LUIGI *pushes sacks under couch.*

Giovanni Push them well out of sight.

Luigi Christ, I didn't think we had this much.

Giovanni It's the yoga effect.

Luigi Course it is.

Giovanni When you look at things upside down.

Luigi What are you on about?

Giovanni When Indians have nothing to eat they stand on their heads and imagine as much food as they can eat.

Luigi Does it help?

Giovanni No. They're still starving.

They stash the coffin in the wardrobe.

Luigi 'Scuse me, mate. (*Stops.*) Funny that.

Giovanni What's that?

Luigi It works.

Giovanni What does?

Luigi That yoga effect. First the food doubles in quantity. Then I get this silly notion that there's an Inspector in the cupboard. Silly old me.

Margherita (*Off.*) Antonia, that's it. I'm going in. Don't blame me if I let it all out.

Giovanni Quick, unlock the bedroom door. (LUIGI *unlocks the door. The men run to the sofa and sit casually. Enter* MARGHERITA.) Margherita! How are you! You look well. Is the baby well?

Margherita Good question. Ah —

Antonia (*Enters.*) What the bloody hell is — Oh. Giovanni! You're back!

Giovanni Yes. I'm back.

Luigi Ha. He's back. See. It's Giovanni.

Antonia And Luigi.
Luigi Yes. Me. Luigi.
Antonia Hello Luigi.
Luigi Hello Antonia.
Antonia How nice.
Margherita I'm here too.
Giovanni You've had it!
Antonia Have I?
Giovanni The transplant.
Luigi The transplant.
Margherita The transplant.
Antonia But only a little bit.
Giovanni Which bit?
Antonia Well. It wasn't big, you know.
Giovanni I knew it. She's such an idiot. She's only gone and done a caesarian!
Antonia Only a little one.
Giovanni How little?
Antonia Little enough to work.
Giovanni You see?!
Luigi And what about you, dear?
Margherita Ah. Yes. I don't know. Antonia?
Luigi What you asking her for? Don't you know?
Antonia How could she, poor little pet. She was under the anaesthetic.
Giovanni Weren't you under the anaesthetic?
Antonia What is this? Some kind of third degree? (*Cupboard door swings open.* GIOVANNI *leans on it.*) And why are you leaning on that door?
Giovanni What door?
Luigi Yes, what door?
Antonia He's leaning against the door. The cupboard door.
Margherita *Our* cupboard door?
Antonia You are leaning.
Giovanni (*Moving away.*) No I'm not.
Antonia I saw you leaning.
Giovanni Post-natal shock Luigi.

Both cupboard doors open. GIOVANNI *and* ANTONIA *lean.*

Antonia What was that?
Luigi What was what?

Sink cupboard door opens. MARGHERITA *leans.*

Luigi What was that?

Front door opens. LUIGI *leans.*

Enter MARGHERITA.

Antonia You're leaning now.
Luigi What me? Ha Ha Ha.

There follows a mad panic-striken circus of doors and windows flying open ending with the collapse of the cuckoo clock in a cloud of feathers.

Giovanni Never mind who's leaning. Who's had the caesarian? Who's had the transplant?
Luigi And who's had the baby?
Antonia Cowards! Not a blessed thought for us. We get up from our sick-beds to be with our husbands in this time of crisis and that's the thanks we get! What should I have done, Giovanni? She was in trouble — about to lose her baby — so I helped her out, didn't I? Don't you always say we should help each other? Luigi, tell him.
Luigi (*Lost for words.*) I'm speechless. Margherita —
Margherita Antonia — You tell him.
Antonia I'm going to cry.
Giovanni No. (*Moves to comfort her.*)
Antonia I'm all right.
Giovanni You look beautiful with that belly. It takes me back.
Antonia I'm going to cry again.
Margherita Me too.
Luigi Is it moving? Can I feel?
Margherita No Luigi!
Luigi It's my baby.
Margherita But it's her belly!
Luigi But we're relatives now.
Giovanni That's right!
Margherita I don't come into this, I suppose? I'm rubbish. A nothing. (*Cries.*)
Antonia How can you treat her like this? Cheer her up. I've got to go out.
Giovanni Are you out of your mind? With all this weather? You'll freeze. Think of the child! Lie down.

Enter OLD MAN, played by the same actor, of course.

Old Man Can I come in?
Giovanni Dad! Come in.
Antonia Hello, Dad.
Giovanni These are my friends. Margherita. Luigi. This is my father.
Luigi and Margherita How do you do?
Luigi Giovanni, did you know your dad looks like —
Giovanni Don't say it. I know. Without a moustache.
Old Man (*To MARGHERITA.*) Antonia how young you're looking.
Giovanni Dad. That's Antonia on the sofa.
Old Man Is she sick? Are you sick?
Giovanni No. She's expecting.
Old Man Who?

Giovanni A child.

Old Man Why? Where's he gone to? Oh you're back already. (*To* LUIGI.) Hello, lad. You shouldn't keep your mother waiting. He's a big lad, ain't he? Oh I've got a letter for you. Sent to me by mistake.

Giovanni Who from?

Old Man The bleeding owner of this block. He says you haven't paid the rent for four months. Here's another letter from the gas, they want their money and so do the electric.

Giovanni What!? Give me those! What is this!? They can take a run, I've always paid my way, haven't I, Antonia?

Antonia Oh yes. Oh yes. We've always paid our way, Dad. I can't understand it for the life of me.

Giovanni They've got it wrong! Definitely. Here, turn the light on, Luigi.

Margherita Oh no.

Luigi On, off, on, off.

Giovanni What's wrong here? Funny. Funny. (*Stops and looks at* ANTONIA.) Antonia, we have paid those bills... Antonia, tell me we've paid!

Antonia Look at him. Screaming at a pregnant woman. Carry on like that and I'll have this baby premature. Then we'll start all over again with the transplants.

Margherita, Luigi and Old Man Oh no.

Luigi Don't do that. Don't let's start —

Giovanni All right. I'll speak softer. Just answer me.

Antonia What was the question?

Giovanni Have we paid the gas and the rent and the electric?

Antonia Oh that question. It's come back to me.

Giovanni Well?

Antonia No.

Giovanni (*Shouting.*) You old cow.

Luigi, Margherita and Old Man (*Pointing to their stomachs in warning.*) SSsssshhhhh!

Giovanni What have I been working all my life for? Tell me that? Eh? (*Shouting.*) Have I been working so I just get cut off —

Margherita, Luigi and Old Man SSsssshhhhh!

Giovanni Sorry. Sorry. Sorry. The baby. Of course. Margherita has paid, Margherita has, haven't you, Margherita? Paid.

Luigi Of course she has. Haven't you, Margherita? Tell him.

Margherita Oh dear. As it happens, I haven't.

Luigi (*Shouting.*) What!

Giovanni, Margherita and Old Man SSssshhhhh!

Antonia Well, now you know. Margherita and me and the other wives on this floor, and on the other floors in the block, and the flats opposite, and come to that all the wives and women in this area are just a bunch of old slags. Instead of paying our gas bills we've been buying jewellery and taking day trips to Rome to buy the latest Paris creations —

Giovanni But why didn't you ask for more money?

Antonia You didn't have any more to ask for. What was the point? Would you have stolen to pay the gas?

Giovanni Never! But why didn't you tell me?

Antonia Why didn't you ask? (*Starts to cry.*)

Old Man Aaah. There there. Everything will turn out for the best.

Giovanni Who says?

Old Man I says.

All SSssssshhhhh!

Old Man Now lay off your wife for a minute.

Antonia Yeah. (*Sob.*) Lay off.

Old Man Anyway, there's always a silver lining. I've brought back all that stuff of yours. So even if you don't have a roof over your head at least you can eat.

Luigi What's he on about?

Margherita Haven't the faintest.

Old Man Yes. You know. All that food and stuff you forgot about in my shed. Well, I've brought it back. Here, I'll bring it in. (*Fetches stuff in from outside the door.*)

Giovanni Dad, you've got it wrong. It's not ours. Antonia. Is it?

Antonia Don't look at me.

Putting shopping bags on kitchen table.

Old Man Well, I never. I saw you coming out of my shed and I thought —

Margherita No!

Luigi What?

Margherita No.

Old Man Well, that is a puzzle, ain't it.

Antonia All right. It's just something I picked up at bargain prices at the supermarket.

Giovanni How bargain?

Antonia Very bargain. Look I only paid half price for half the stuff and the other half I half nicked.

Luigi What's she talking about?

Giovanni Nicked? Have you started nicking now?

Antonia Yes, I have.

Margherita No, she hasn't!

Antonia It's no use, Margherita. They had to find out.

Giovanni I can't get over it. I'm going barmy. My wife a tea leaf.

Luigi Yeah, well. It's not that barmy. Let's have less of the moral indignation. (*Pointing under couch.*)

Giovanni Why not? I'm entitled. It's all right for you, but I'm up to here in debt due to this totally irresponsible tea leaf here.

Antonia That's it. Call me a thief. And what about 'whore' while you're at it? (*Undoes belly, revealing shopping bag.*) All this ain't a kid. It's veg, and spag and rice and sugar and spag and spaghetti. All of it nicked.

Luigi (*Peering in and under shopping bag.*) What happened to the kid? The transplant?

Giovanni The baby tent? The fully automatic —

Luigi Belt up for once. Margherita?

Margherita Yes??

Luigi (*Thinks, looks at* MARGHERITA *and* ANTONIA.) It's all a con. The whole thing.

Giovanni To think I was worried to death about your health. The whole thing was a pack of lies.

Luigi Even me being a father.

Antonia Yeah. It's all lies. The whole thing.

Giovanni I'm not half going to give you one. (*Starting towards* ANTONIA.)

Luigi Don't be hasty. (*Holding him back.*)

Giovanni All right I won't. I'll kill her slowly. I'll mangle her into little pieces.

Old Man Well, I'm off. I think you've had all the news. Look after yourself. Ta ra.

They all wave politely.

Giovanni Ta ta.

Luigi Yes. Nice to have met you.

OLD MAN *exits.*

Giovanni Right, let me at her.

LUIGI *again restrains* GIOVANNI *with difficulty.*

Antonia Let him go, Luigi. Let him kill me. I'll just sit here and let him whack my brains out. I'm tired of this shitty life. I'm tired of all the running around trying to scratch a living out of nothing with no help at all. All you get from him is moral indignati...

Luigi Indignation.

Antonia Yes. That. And a lot of wind. Our kids are chucked on the scrapheap, a whole generation of them without the hope of getting a job. The right laying waste and who's standing up to them? Him and his party. Like a dead haddock. I've had enough of it. Luigi. I've changed my mind. I'm not giving in. Don't let him go after all.

Luigi Oh, all right. (*Grabs* GIOVANNI.)

Antonia I'm leaving home instead.

Luigi That's good.

Antonia I'm going to live round your place, Luigi.

Luigi That's bad.

Margherita Help!

Giovanni You can't leave. You're my wife.

Luigi See?

Giovanni Keep out of this! She's my wife.

Antonia I'm your wife. But are you my husband?

Giovanni What are you on about?

Antonia Well, you're not the bloke I married, that's for certain. You're not the Giovanni I knew. You were a fighter then. Don't rock the boat. Where's the real Giovanni Bardi? Millet soup!

Giovanni All right, if that's what you feel. Go on. Go and leave and live at Luigi's. And take the bleeding sugar with you.

Antonia What?

Giovanni Yeah. Might sweeten you up a bit. And the rice and the flour.

Antonia What's he talking about?

Giovanni It's under the sofa. We nicked it today.

Margherita No that's our stuff. We nicked it.

Luigi No. He's right. We nicked it. Three sacks worth.

ANTONIA *pulls sack from under couch.*

Antonia You blooming old hypocrite. 'I'd rather starve than eat stolen food.' You two-faced sodbox.

Giovanni Leave it out.

Antonia Well, I'm well out of it. Let's go, Luigi, Margherita. (*Exits.*)

Luigi Don't let's be hasty.

Giovanni Just because you're right you don't have to stand around gloating. Go on, the lot of you.

Luigi (*Calling down the hall.*) Hear him out, Antonia, you might change your mind.

Margherita Yeah!!

Re-enter ANTONIA.

Antonia Wait a minute. Did you say 'because you're right'?

Giovanni You heard. I'm not going to repeat myself.

Antonia Are you feeling all right?

Giovanni No I'm not. I feel sick.

Antonia What about?

Giovanni About today. About tomorrow.

Antonia What are you on about?

Giovanni None of your business.

Antonia Suit yourself.

Giovanni It's the women today and Luigi on the train with Marco and Tonino and the youngsters in the canteen (and even the shop stewards) and the guys at the lorry with the sacks of flour and rice.

Luigi Anybody you left out?

Giovanni Yeah me.

Luigi You don't come into it.

Antonia He does.

Giovanni No. I don't. That's it. That's what gets me in the goolies.

Luigi See?

Giovanni What were the women doing?

Luigi Nicking.

Giovanni No they weren't.

Antonia He will argue.

Giovanni They were making a stand. Where've I been all my life? I don't know. I'm confused.

Luigi No? Really?

Giovanni Alright! Twenty years Luigi. Twenty years to learn what I've learnt.

Antonia And what have you learnt?

Giovanni I don't know!

Luigi You are a slow learner.

Giovanni Sneer you may. But I've fell in. (*Tapping temple.*) That's what I've done. Fell in, finally. All those people today milling about the streets with groceries up their jumpers are looking for a bit of leadership, that's what. They're saying, 'Get in there, old cock, there's a fight on.' And they're saying it to their unions. The right are on the rampage and they're saying, 'We've had a bellyful of it' and they're saying, 'If you don't take hold, we will!' And they're saying to the politicians, 'We want the bread *and* the biscuits, so shut your cake'ole!'. And us, the so-called opposition, is wobbling in its boots. Well, we're going to have to pull ourselves up by the bootstraps, and roll our sleeves up and get weaving up to our elbows otherwise someone'll nick the carpet out from under our feet and we'll be up the spout without a paddle.

Pause.

Margherita I know exactly what I mean.

Giovanni Yes, well. Buzz off, the lot of you. I've got some thinking to do.

Antonia What about?

Giovanni About today. About you.

Antonia Are you asking me to stay?

Luigi I think he is. Aren't you, Giovanni?

Margherita I think he is, too.

Giovanni I didn't say that.

Antonia Well, I will.

Giovanni You will?

Antonia Course I will. Don't argue.

Giovanni I'm not arguing. I was just —

Antonia Oh belt up. Give us a kiss.

They kiss.

Margherita Innit lovely?

Luigi It won't last.

Knocking.

Margherita Oh my God!

Luigi Who is it?
Inspector Police! Open up!
Antonia Quick, hide everything!
Margherita Aaaaaaooouuu!
Antonia Dozy cow!

General panic as they run hither and thither concealing everything.

Giovanni Hold it. Hold everything. What is this? They've been giving us the run around all day. I'm not running any more. We'll face the bastards.
Inspector (*Entering from cupboard.*) I can see! I can see! St Evlalia be praised. Merciful Saint! And look at me. I'm pregnant! Oh what a bonus. I'm a mother! I'm a mother.
Giovanni What's got into him?

Pause. They look at each other.

Antonia There's only one thing for it, Margherita. We'll sing the song.

They sing the song (vocal and instrumental depending on the cast's musical talents).

Sebben che siamo donne
Paura non abbiamo
Per amori dei nostri figli
In legge ci mettiamo

E voi altri signorini
Che ci avette tanto orgoglio
Abbassate la superbia
E apriti il porta foglio

They say we should be moderate
Not stirring up class war
But we're bent on being obdurate
We'll take it all we don't ask more

We'll defeat their aims for starters
We'll foil their dastardly plan
Can we have their guts for garters?
We say fucking right we can!

Fade to blackout.

END OF PLAY

Methuen Modern Plays

include work by